CW01080654

SURVIVOR'S LEAVE

OTHER BOOKS BY
ROBERT SUTHERLAND

Mystery at Black Rock Island (Scholastic, 1983)

The Loon Lake Murders (Scholastic, 1987)

Son of the Hounds (Scholastic, 1988)

The Fugitive (Celebrate, USA, 1988)

The Ghost of Ramshaw Castle (Scholastic, 1990)

Suddenly a Spy (Scholastic, 1992)

Death Island (Scholastic, 1994)

If Two Are Dead (Scholastic, 1997)

The Secret of Devil Lake (HarperCollins, 1998)

A River Apart (Fitzhenry & Whiteside, 2000)

The Adventures of Tommy Smith (HarperCollins, 2003)

Greysteel's Ghost (HarperCollins, 2005)

The Schooner's Revenge (HarperCollins, 2008)

SURVIVOR'S LEAVE

ROBERT SUTHERLAND

RONSDALE PRESS

SURVIVOR'S LEAVE
Copyright © 2010 Robert Sutherland

RONSDALE PRESS
3350 West 21st Avenue, Vancouver, B.C., Canada V6S 1G7
www.ronsdalepress.com

Typesetting: Julie Cochrane, in Minion 12 pt on 16
Cover Art & Design: Nancy de Brouwer, Alofli Graphic Design
Paper: Ancient Forest Friendly "Silva" (FSC) — 100% post-consumer waste,
    totally chlorine-free and acid-free

Ronsdale Press wishes to thank the following for their support of its publishing program: the Canada Council for the Arts, the Government of Canada through the Book Publishing Industry Development Program (BPIDP), the British Columbia Arts Council, and the Province of British Columbia through the British Columbia Book Publishing Tax Credit program.

Library and Archives Canada Cataloguing in Publication

Sutherland, Robert, 1925–
    Survivor's leave / Robert Sutherland.

ISBN 978-1-55380-097-2

I. World War, 1939–1945 — Juvenile fiction. I. Title.

PS8587.U798S95 2010   jC813'.54   C2009-906132-5

At Ronsdale Press we are committed to protecting the environment. To this end we are working with Markets Initiative (www.oldgrowthfree.com) and printers to phase out our use of paper produced from ancient forests. This book is one step towards that goal.

Printed in Canada by Marquis Printing, Quebec

for Lottie,
my war bride,
with love

PART ONE

The North Sea and HMCS *Loch Lyon*

PART TWO

Croydon and Doodlebug Alley

PART THREE

Penraven and the Bottle Dungeon

PART ONE
The North Sea and HMCS *Loch Lyon*
(Summer 1944)

Chapter One

"TAKING WATER! BOTTOM plates and floor plates buckled."

The distress call went out, seeking the ears of the commodore in command of the sixty-ship convoy bound for Murmansk. Hundreds of tons of war materials en route for the hungry war machines of the beleaguered Soviets were in the holds of that convoy. All available escort ships would be needed to bring them safely through the blockade that would be thrown up by the Nazi U-boats and aircraft determined to interrupt the convoy's passage north of Norway. And now the distress call went out from one of those escort vessels, the frigate HMCS *Loch Lyon*.

This was the worst weather the *Loch Lyon* had met in her

brief career. The seas were mountainous, rushing before a fierce wind that had ice on its breath. The waves pounded the ship ceaselessly, they rolled over her, lifting her, then rushed on to drop her into black, frothing caverns, with a crash that jarred the teeth of her watchmen.

Water was ankle deep in the mess deck, and anything that was not properly stowed was sloshing about. This was not caused by the buckled plates. They were down below. The very bottom plates had given way first, then the floor plates in the magazine. Pumps were working on that. But in spite of battened hatches the raging seas were not to be denied and salt water was everywhere.

Able Seaman Glen Cassley had left the mess deck, dogging the hatch behind him, to take his turn as look-out. He staggered across the heaving deck that dropped away from his reaching foot to throw him against the bulkhead, then came up and knocked him to his knees. He crawled to the ladder that led to the upper deck. Once he was outside, the wind hit him like the blow from a heavyweight boxing glove. He grasped the lifeline stretched across and above the deck, shielding his face as best he could from the stinging spray, and worked his way aft. His lookout station was on the quarterdeck, but that was continuously under water. No one could stay there.

Instead, he made his way to the gun deck. Here was the Pom-Pom, a four-barrel gun that took its fanciful name from the steady *pom pom pom* as she hurled two-pounder shells against the foe. But it was neither U-boats nor aircraft that was the enemy now. It was the weather, and no weapon could protect the frigate from that.

Glen couldn't even protect his face from the stinging spray and biting wind. It found its way into and under his oilskin coat and hood. He gave up trying to shield his face as he searched the heaving wastes for some sign of the convoy. It would be scattered now, over hundreds of miles of ocean, every ship for itself in its fight against the elements. The *Loch Lyon* wouldn't be the only casualty. Some ancient tramp steamers, dragged out of retirement in the desperate battle of the Atlantic, would succumb to the merciless pounding and head, hopefully, for the nearest shelter, hoping to live and fight another day.

When the weather eventually cleared, the escort ships' first task would be to round up the scattered ships and form them into defendable convoy again. But it looked as if the *Loch Lyon* would not be a part of that . . .

The merchant ships might be lost in the murk where heavy clouds dragged ragged hemlines across the towering waves, but the nearest escort ship, HMCS *Annan*, should be out there, not too far away. She had been there a few minutes ago, her signal lamp blinking, a pitching, heaving grey shape barely distinguishable in a grey world. He searched for some sign of her. But she was gone. Disappeared. He caught his breath, his numb hands clutching his binoculars . . .

There she was! Like a whale surfacing, climbing out of a

cavern deeper than a grave, throwing a cloud of spume higher than her masthead, rolling far over, then righting herself, slowly, fighting the screaming elements, just as was the *Loch Lyon* . . .

But the *Loch Lyon* had lost the fight. Bruised and battered, her pumps fighting to control the invading sea, she had to abandon the convoy and head for shelter.

Chapter Two

"HAVE YOU HEARD the latest scuttlebutt?"

"No. What's the latest?"

Glen had fought his way back to the mess deck at the end of his watch. The tables and benches, clamped to the deck, were vacated. The sailors off watch had sought relief from the sickening motion of the ship in their hammocks. These were slung overhead, so close together that now and then they bumped each other, but their movement was soothing compared to the frenetic gyrations of the deck. Glen had removed his life jacket and sea boots and hoisted himself into his own "mick," inevitably disturbing his neighbour in doing so. Arthur "Ding Dong" Bell — or "Ding" for short — had given him a brief grimace, then had asked him about the rumours. Somehow, no one knew how, rumours spread through the lower deck almost before the authorities on the bridge knew about them. Sometimes they were correct.

"No," said Glen, pulling in the sides of his hammock so that it was as if he were in a cocoon, "what's the latest?" It was only because their hammocks touched that they were able to hear each other above the clamour of the storm, the shrieking of the wind, the pounding of the seas, the hiss of spray beyond the thin bulkhead.

"We're heading for dry dock, for repairs to our bottom."

"I guessed that much. What dry dock?"

"You'll never guess this. The nearest available dry dock is in London!"

"London! No kidding!" Glen would have sat up in excitement if the contours of his hammock permitted it. "Who says so? You can't be sure."

"The Buffer says so. At least the Quartermaster *says* the Buffer says so and that's good enough for me. The East India docks, to be exact. I thought that meant we'd be going to the East Indies, but no. That's what they call the docks in the east end of London. Don't ask me why."

London! Glen grinned. "Imagine, Ding! One moment we're heading for death and destruction on the Murmansk run, then the next we're heading for London! Never say anything against North Atlantic gales again in my hearing."

"Yeah. Well, don't forget London's the favourite target of the Luftwaffe."

"*Was*," corrected Glen. "Since the invasion they've been too busy protecting their homeland to pay much attention to London." He stopped, catching his breath. A mountainous sea had evidently borne down on the *Lock Lyon*, rolling her far over then dropping her like a stone into a moving canyon, jarring her, driving her as if against a brick wall. The deck head that should have been only inches above his face seemed to tip until it was almost beside him. It was weird. In his hammock he was almost steady, just a soothing motion bumping him gently against that of his friend. He gripped the sides of his hammock, waiting, tense. Somewhere overhead something came loose and rolled across the heaving deck, battering against a bulkhead . . .

"I hope that's not a depth charge," said Ding Dong grimly. "And I'm glad I'm not on watch. Someone's going to have a dicey time securing that, no matter what it is."

"Yeah." Glen waited, listening, half expecting a summons to the deck, but none came. The fewer men on deck at the mercy of the raging seas the better. He realized that. Some other poor chap had to try to secure whatever it was, while clinging to a lifeline. He waited, breathless, then realized that the battering noise had ceased.

"They've got it," he said. "Either secured it or lost it over the side."

"If it was a depth charge and it's gone over the side we'll know soon enough. And if it's on shallow setting, we'll be going down to see Davy Jones instead of the East India docks in London."

Glen nodded, holding his breath. A depth charge designed to damage, if not destroy a U-boat would make short work of the already weakened bottom plates of the frigate.

But nothing happened. For a moment neither spoke, silent in relief. Then Ding Dong said, "So why are you anxious to go to London?"

"I have friends there."

"Friends? In London? How come? You've been there before the war?"

"No. A pen pal. Our teacher at school arranged for each of us interested to correspond with a boy or girl in the British Isles. I got one in London. Croydon, to be exact. A suburb of London. We've been writing back and forth for I guess three years now."

"Which is it? A boy or girl?"

"Sorry to disappoint you. A boy. Named Jack. But he has two sisters. Very pretty girls they are too."

"Ah! Now you're talking! If you get time off to go and see them, how about taking me along?"

"Sure, but probably not much use. Jack's joined the air force and last I heard the girls had joined up too, as soon as they were seventeen. So I guess the only people at home will be their parents. Still, I want to meet them, and, you never know, Jack may be on leave."

"What's he do in the air force?"

"He was training as a gunner. Air crew. Must be through now, so he's probably in one of those massive air strikes against Germany we hear about."

"And the girls? Air force for them too?"

"Probably. I'm not sure. Want to see a picture of them?"

"You have a picture? You've been holding out on us. You're supposed to share pictures of your girlfriends, you know."

"They're not my girlfriends. I never wrote to *them* — either of them. The picture's in my locker. You'll have to wait till I feel like getting down there and finding it."

"So what did you write about then, you and Jack what's-his-name?"

"Barclay. Oh, lots of things. He lives in a huge city — probably the greatest city in the world if you have any British blood in your veins. And I live in a village, population of one hundred and fifty, counting cats and dogs. The country, the climate, the schools, the sports. He plays soccer and cricket. I play football and hockey. Lots to write about. Girls never came into it."

"Girls always come into it," asserted Ding Dong. "Still, he sent you their picture."

"It's a family picture. Mum and Dad, Jack, Heather and Susan Barclay. The girls are twins."

"Well, don't forget, you're going to show me the picture. D'you think we'll get any leave when we're in London?"

"Overnight liberty anyway if we're not duty watch. Maybe more, depending on how long it takes the dockyard mateys to fix us up. I have some leave due me. If I can wrangle a week that would be perfect." He hesitated as another sea rolled the ship far over. "I'm assuming, of course, that we're going to survive long enough to get to London."

Chapter Three

SOMEWHERE, AT SOME unmarked line, the waters of the Norwegian Sea merge with those of the North Sea. By the time the *Loch Lyon* reached the area, the winds had lost their viciousness, the seas were less mountainous. The plunge into black, moving caverns, the jarring smash into walls of water no longer threatened to do more damage to the bottom plates. A long swell bearing down on her starboard quarter caused her to roll sickeningly but increased her speed so that she was able to maintain a safe, steady ten knots.

At this speed, the trip to London should be a leisurely cruise — or so Glen Cassley thought. He was wrong.

In the morning watch, as bos'n's mate, Glen was in the wheel-house, his hands gripping the wheel. Here, the ship was in his hands. He had control of both the direction and speed in which the *Loch Lyon* sailed. Not for the first time the incongruity of the situation hit him. The ship was in his hands, yet he was a very new sailor, having lived his life a thousand or so miles from the ocean, and he had been in the navy less than a year. At the touch of the wheel he could send the ship off in a new direction. Not only that but he could increase or decrease the speed of the ship. Indeed, he could switch from full ahead to full astern and everything in between at the simple moving of the handle of the engine room telegraph right there beside him. The ship was in his inexperienced hands, yet he couldn't even see where she was going. Three feet in front of him was a solid bulkhead.

Oh, sometimes he could see where the ship *was* at that moment. Weather and the time of day permitting, the scuttle might be open and he could see through the porthole. He could do so now, seeing the long, rolling swell sweeping by, feeling it tugging at the wheel, so that he had to fight against it to hold the ship on course.

And sometimes, weather permitting, the door behind him was open. Today he could look past the funnel, the gun deck, the quarterdeck where the depth charge racks held their drums of death, to the wake, writhing at the whim of the swell. Yes, he could see where the ship had been, where it was now. But he could not see ahead.

The answer to all this, of course, was the mouthpiece of the speaking tube inches from his face. At the other end of the tube was the officer of the watch. *His* view was unrestricted. He was up there on the wide open bridge, without even a roof over his head. He could see all around. At every corner of the ship were look-outs with powerful binoculars in touch with him constantly. His radar operators could see far beyond the horizon. His asdic operators could "see" into the depths of the ocean. His signalmen sent and received messages from the ships in the convoy. The wireless operators kept him in touch with the Admiralties in London and Ottawa.

And perhaps as important as all these, the officer of the watch had experience, or he wouldn't be in command. Yes, he had all this, but there was one thing — no, two things — he did not have. He had neither the steering wheel nor the engine room telegraph. For the correct operation of these vital instruments he depended on an inexperienced nineteen-year-old.

In fact, thought Glen, in spite of the disparity in our situations we're mutually dependent. I depend on him giving me the correct orders. He depends on me carrying them out . . .

"Bridge wheelhouse." The voice over the tube was loud. "Slow ahead. Right full rudder."

"Slow ahead. Right full rudder on, sir." He swung the engine room telegraph from half ahead to slow, and swung the wheel to starboard, watching the ship's head on the gyro compass come round, felt the ship plunge drunkenly as the swell hit her broadside.

"Meet her. Steer three-ten."

"Meet her. Steer three-ten sir." He swung the wheel back until the ship's head steadied, then on to the course requested.

"Who's on the wheel?"

Glen gulped. Was his reaction to the orders too slow? "Able Seaman Cassley, sir."

But he needn't have worried. "Right, Cassley. The Cox'n will be relieving you shortly. We'll be going to action stations."

"Action stations." The words, usually accompanied by the blaring of a Klaxon designed to jolt the sleepiest sailor out of his hammock, had lost much of their tension as far as Glen was concerned. At its sound, like everyone, he still made a mad dash for his station. But he no longer expected to be battling a lurking U-boat or seeking an attacking German aircraft in the sights of his gun every time "action stations" sounded. There had been too many such calls that had fizzled out to nothing. An asdic contact that the operator believed *could* be from the hull of a submarine, turned out to be nothing more than a school of fish — sometimes confirmed by dead or stunned fish floating belly up — or from the hull of an uncharted wreck, one of the many that littered the ocean floor.

A few minutes — or maybe even hours — searching, dropping depth charges or squids, then the seemingly inevitable turning away to rejoin the convoy, with the officer of the watch inscribing in the log the simple "classified non-sub."

That it would be more of the same this time, he had no doubt. The casual way in which the officer on the bridge had said that he would shortly be sounding action stations certainly suggested that it was no emergency.

That seemed to be confirmed when the cox'n arrived at the wheelhouse. He was a bearded chief petty officer who had joined the navy before Glen had been born.

"You heard from the bridge? I'm to relieve you. Carry on to your action station."

Glen nodded, relinquishing the wheel. "What's up, Chief?"

The Cox'n shrugged. "Who knows? A contact. Maybe asdic, maybe radar. We'll soon know."

If *he* doesn't know, thought Glen, I can't expect anyone to tell a mere able seaman. He was climbing the ladder to the after gun deck when the raucous alarm horn sounded.

In a matter of minutes the ship was cleared for action. Deep in her belly below the water line the stokers stood to their engines. The stewards and cooks, barred from the flooded magazine, their standard post, stood by the ammunition hoists below and ready-use lockers on deck. The cox'n took over in the wheelhouse, senior operators were in charge in the wireless, asdic and radar cabins, the gunners and depth charge men stood to their weapons, the yeoman of signals was on the bridge. The "Old Man" was in command.

Glen's action station was in the cockpit of the port twin Oerlikon gun on the after-gun deck. Ding was his loader, standing by to take the magazines of twenty-millimetre shells from the ready-use locker when needed. The two-man crew of the starboard twin were at their station on the other side.

"What's up?" Nobody knew.

Glen slipped into the cockpit, donned his earphones and mouthpiece.

"Port twin closed up," he reported to the gunnery officer on the bridge.

"Very good. Stand by."

"What's he say?" asked Ding eagerly.

"Very good. Stand by. What did you expect? Never mind. 'Guns' will be around soon to fill us in, unless it's real urgent, and it doesn't seem to be."

Sure enough, Lieutenant Walker, the gunnery officer, arrived a few minutes later. It was his custom to check personally on all the gun posts when action stations was sounded.

"Everything in order, Cassley?"

"Aye aye, sir. Closed up ready for action. Can you tell us what's going on? Do we have a contact?"

"Not yet, but we're hoping."

"Hoping?" That was unusual. They were always "hoping" for a contact with the enemy of course, but hope was hardly cause for action stations.

"That's right. An aircraft on coastal patrol spotted a sub on the surface twelve miles or so east of us. Dropped one depth bomb without effect but couldn't hang around. They were just about out of fuel. The sub dived, of course."

"About twelve miles? And we're doing what, about ten knots? Not much hope is there, sir? She's not going to hang around waiting for us."

Lieutenant Walker chuckled. "That's true, of course. But there *is* a chance. She's most likely a brand new boat out of the shipyards at Hamburg or Bremen. Her position and direction support that guess. And if that's correct she'll be heading for the gap between the Orkneys and the Shetlands. We're hoping she's doing that and will continue to do so. If so, we may be able to intercept her."

Ding looked skeptical. "D'you really think we have a hope, sir?"

The officer shrugged. "It's worth a try. And this time we won't have a convoy to worry about."

Glen knew what he meant. He thought back to the time when a convoy travelling from Gibraltar to Plymouth had been attacked at night. Radar had picked up an echo several miles away. A star shell illumined the scene, and there was a U-boat on the surface, moments before it dived, the first and only one Glen had seen. That time they had known for sure, as the frigate headed for the site, that the asdic echo came from the hull of an enemy submarine. So often an echo had been false. How many depth charges had been wasted on schools of fish or an uncharted wreck? But not this time!

And then the word had come through. *That* U-boat was no longer a menace. It was too far away to catch up. They were to leave it and rejoin the threatened convoy.

That, he reflected, was the purpose of an escort ship. It was *not* simply to get from port A to port B, or even to destroy the enemy. Its duty was to "ensure the safe and timely arrival of the convoy." The convoy was all-important. The escort ships were expendable.

But this time there was no convoy to worry about.

Submarines travelled on the surface as long as possible, to save their batteries and for the increased speed. At the best of times their small silhouettes were not easily picked up on the radar screen, and today the long, rolling swell created deep furrows that could hide a U-boat while the watch on her bridge could detect the mast of a frigate miles away. In that case she could dive before she was close enough to register on the radar or the asdic and change direction out of danger. But, as Lieutenant Wallace said, there was a chance . . .

Chapter Four

MINUTES PASSED. THERE was no telling how many. Glen used the time to sweep the faceless sea through his binoculars. There was nothing but the white-flecked rolling seas while the mast traced lazy arcs against the leaden skies.

Then the loudspeaker broke the silence.

"Attention all hands. A radar contact has vanished well astern but we have an asdic echo. Stand by."

Glen adjusted his ear phones, nodding to his loader. "I can hear it . . . "

Then no earphones were needed. The sound increased until it could be heard all over the ship. *Ping*. A moment of silence, then *ping* again. Another pause, shorter, then it came again. *Ping . . . ping . . . ping.*

Was it another school of fish? Or another uncharted wreck? No, not that. It was moving. Was it a U-boat, taking evasive action?

Ping ping ping. Louder, closer together. Tension grew on the gun deck. Was it a U-boat? It couldn't be the one that had registered on the radar screen. That was too far away. Could there be two of them, sailing in tandem, bent on breaking out into the happy hunting grounds of the North Atlantic?

Except for the insistent pinging, the ship was silent, as if sniffing the electric air. There was just the quiet voice of the asdic operator, his directions relayed to the helmsman; then the muffled clang of the engine room telegraph reducing speed to a crawl. *Ping ping . . .*

There would be sweat pouring down the faces of the stokers in their engine room, only a thin shell of steel between them and the waiting ocean. There would be cold sweat on the faces of the depth charge crews, and the men standing by at the "squid" mortars, ready for the word to fire. Only if their efforts were successful would Glen and the gun crews be called on to do their part. Meanwhile they waited, while the steady *ping-ping* grew louder, more insistent.

Ping ping ping. Almost continuous. Then a new sound.

Phoom-phoom-phoom. Phoom-phoom-phoom. In rapid succession the two three-barrel mortars, called "squids," hurled their projectiles over the fo'c'stle to splash into the sea ahead of the ship. A long moment of tense silence, then the explosion. A crash against the hull, rocking her. A towering plume of water high in the air, blossoming and falling. A seething mass of boiling water, and then, yes, there it was. Oil, slowly spreading.

A ripple of excitement ran through the ship's company. But no one was disillusioned. This was no proof yet that there was an enemy submarine down there. It could still be a school of fish, and the oil from a long abandoned wreck. But there were no stunned or dead fish covering the surface. Just that oil slick. Surely there must be a U-boat down there, perhaps damaged.

Or perhaps not. There was another possibility. U-boat skippers were known to release oil, in the hope that the surface vessel would conclude that the boat had been damaged or destroyed, and would take off after the convoy and leave her to her own devices. But not this time. There was no convoy to protect. The *Loch Lyon* was free to hang around as long as she wished.

The frigate was picking up speed, leaving the tell-tale oil slick behind. But she was not leaving. There was the insistent *ping ping* again, moving, dodging. The *Loch Lyon* swung around, 180 degrees, moving fast, a white froth in her wake, her bow slicing the water, her wash rolling and breaking. Then, when the pings were loud, almost continuous, the order was given. Three depth charges rolled off her stern.

Two more arced high in the air, one from each side, to fall in the water. A long moment of tense waiting as the ship hurried on, away from the scene, mindful of her own weakened bottom plates. Then she swung around, just as the underwater explosions smacked against her hull, and the surface erupted, great geysers of tortured water hurled into the air, blossoming, sparkling in a hundred dancing rainbows, then subsiding reluctantly into the churning sea.

The frigate had slowed, and sat there, poised, waiting. Everyone who was in a position to do so stood and held his breath and waited. There was a U-boat down there. This time there was no doubt. She must have been damaged. But was it enough? Every gun on board that could be brought to bear on the scene swung round and waited.

And then, at last, they saw it. First the nose breaking the surface, then, further back, the periscope, the anti-aircraft guns, the conning tower. Now they could see the big gun on the deck ahead of the conning tower as the black hull lay full out on the surface, rolling in the swell. And men poured from the hatches, manning the anti-aircraft guns, dashing for the deck gun.

There was no need for the order to fire. With a jolt of excitement, of disbelief that the moment for action had finally come, Glen swung his gun around till he found the U-boat in his sights and he squeezed his trigger and watched tracer arc towards the enemy. There were men over there. He was shooting at them. He tried not to think of that. It was the U-boat, that black underwater monster, he was trying to destroy. The pompom was firing too, the heavy thump thump of the four barrels pouring their two-pounder shells at the U-boat. And then the earsplitting crash of the four-inch up forward. There could be no doubt of the result. She was so close the guns could not miss.

But the submarine was not giving up without a fight. Her guns were firing too. Glen heard shells pass overhead in a whistling rush, then shrapnel rattled against the gun shield.

"Get down, Ding!"

The U-boat's deck gun spoke, once, briefly, the shell thudding into the *Lyon's* hull, a sheet of flame, the cry of someone hit by shrapnel, then the sub's deck gun went over the side as the four-inch found the mark.

The conning tower of the sub was being torn to shreds. All her guns fell silent. She began to roll.

"Cease firing. Let go the mid Carley float."

That, Glen guessed, would be for the few German survivors leaving their doomed craft. They would have to look out for themselves. The *Lyon* had something else to worry about.

Glen heard the report from the asdic cabin. "Contact bearing . . . " He didn't catch the bearing. A moment later the same voice, "contact lost" And then another report from the radar operator. "Object bearing . . . " And it was the same bearing.

Another U-boat, surfacing.

"Damage control report."

"Medical Officer report."

"Right full rudder. Full ahead both."

The orders came in quickly, calmly.

The *Loch Lyon* seemed to gather herself in, heel far over, her screws churning the water into a frenzied turmoil as she left the sinking U-boat to its fate.

"Stand by, all hands. We have another submarine on the surface . . . "

The asdic operator again, calm but hurried. "Torpedo running. Bearing . . . "

Torpedo! Glen caught his breath. He was aware of Ding beside him, hand on his shoulder. "She's fired a torpedo at us . . . "

The *Lyon* would be heading directly towards the enemy ship to present the smallest possible target for a regular torpedo. But this type of torpedo didn't need a target.

It would be an acoustic torpedo, one that didn't have to be aimed, that would automatically head for the loudest noise — the racing screws of the *Loch Lyon*. The frigate had one defence. A depth charge was kept ready for such an emergency, set shallow.

The command, urgent. "Let go Anti-Nat charge."

The sailor in control on the quarterdeck acted instantly. A depth charge rolled off the stern. Luckily the frigate was going at full speed. Would it be enough?

A long moment of suspended breath, then a blast, a

double blast as both the depth charge and the torpedo blew simultaneously. The frigate acted like a bucking bronco kicking her stern high, then collapsing with a crash, jarring everything and everyone.

Glen was held firmly in his cockpit but Ding was thrown against the gun, collapsing to the deck.

"Ding! Are you okay?"

"Yeah, I guess." Ding Dong struggled up, nursing his arm. "But what do you suppose that did to our bottom plates?"

For a moment apparently no one had time to think about that.

From their position on the gun deck, Glen and Ding were unable to see ahead. Apparently the second U-boat was visible to those on the bridge and the four-inch gun platform.

"Fire!" The earsplitting crash of the gun. Short. "Up four hundred. Fire!"

"She's diving. Stand by, the squid."

But there would be no further use for the squid mortars. Suddenly the engines were silent.

The *Loch Lyon* slowed, wallowing heavily to a stop.

"Engine room — bridge." Glen heard the report over his earphones. "We're flooding, sir. That blast did it. The bottom plates are done for."

"Very well." Calm acceptance from the captain. "Thanks, Chief. Get your men out."

A moment of silence, then the tannoy, heard throughout the ship.

"All hands on deck. Prepare to abandon ship. Gunners and look-outs stay closed up. There's another sub out there. She's submerged hard on the port bow. Keep a sharp eye out for a periscope."

Another sub, and the *Loch Lyon* was now a sitting duck, dead in the water, rolling slightly to the whim of the sea. The sub wouldn't have to surface to fire a torpedo at this unmoving target. But she might not know, might be concerned only with escape. That was the *Loch Lyon*'s only hope.

Glen sat in his cockpit, eyes searching the surface for an elusive periscope. If the sub came up to periscope depth and recognized what had happened, their fate was sealed. So they waited, and prayed. And time passed, ever so slowly, until they began to breathe more easily.

"She's gone," said Glen at last. "Must have, by now. If she only knew what she's missed."

"Doesn't make much difference," said Ding. "We're going down anyway. Look."

He pointed over the side. The water was climbing up the flanks of the ship, already reaching for the low well deck, the quarterdeck.

"It'd make a difference all right," said Glen. "The difference of quite a few lives. Maybe yours and mine."

"Yeah, I guess. Listen!" Ding was looking eagerly skyward. "A plane! It's got to be one of ours. The sub won't dare surface with a plane about."

His observation was confirmed a few minutes later. "This

is the captain speaking. All hands, prepare to abandon ship. Lower away all boats and floats. There is a destroyer on the way from Scapa. Thank you all, and good luck."

Glen struggled out of his cockpit. "You know what this means, Ding? Survivor's Leave. We qualify for Survivor's Leave! And with any luck we won't even get our feet wet. Maybe I'll get to meet the Barclays after all. You still want to come?"

"Maybe. If the leave's long enough I may get home to Canada. If not, sure I'll come with you. And hope to meet your pal's sisters."

Only a short distance away, on board the submarine U-555, the captain turned away from the periscope and barked orders. He was not about to waste a torpedo on an obviously sinking ship. The U-555 had a more important mission. There was a strange-looking package in her torpedo room she was on orders to deliver. It was marked "Penraven."

PART TWO
Croydon and Doodlebug Alley

Chapter One

HIS MAJESTY'S CANADIAN SHIP *Niobe* was not a ship at all. She was what was known as a "stone frigate" — a barracks, miles from the ocean, in the hills above the Scottish town of Greenock. What had formerly been a home for the mentally challenged was a rambling brick building strung out over acres of ground. There were countless chimney pots indicating the presence of as many fireplaces, which attempted either to warm the "inmates" or smoke them out.

It was a "manning depot" — a temporary home for sailors on the move, those on draft to ships built in Britain, those awaiting transfer, survivors awaiting disposal — and in addition, of course, the staff required to handle all the paperwork involved. Glen and Ding had both been at *Niobe* before. Drafted from Halifax in Canada, sailing on the troopship *Ile de France*, they had arrived at *Niobe* to await a posting to one of the new loch-class frigates built in Britain. They had been only two weeks in barracks before being drafted to the shipyards at Wall's End, near Newcastle, where HMCS *Loch Lyon* had been newly commissioned. Less than a year at sea and now they were back at *Niobe*, their ship at the bottom of the North Sea and one U-boat fewer to harass the convoys.

There was a new air of confidence and hope at the base. The invasion of Europe was a week old now, and Allied troops were securing their hold on the mainland and advancing slowly but surely eastward. Not that there was any doubt about the ferocity of the war at sea. The U-boats would be more anxious than ever to prevent supplies and troops from crossing the Atlantic, but more and more of them were being destroyed with fewer and fewer successes. It was just a matter of time.

They didn't know it at *Niobe*, of course, but the Germans had one more secret weapon to throw at the long suffering people of Britain . . .

The crew of the *Loch Lyon* had been dispersed in various directions. Most were returned to Canada on one of the troop ships to barracks or ships there, after enjoying what was called "Survivor's Leave." Not so Glen and Ding and the other anti-aircraft gunners. A new aircraft carrier was under construction and nearing completion in Belfast, to be turned over to the Canadian navy for service in the far east. She was going to need many gunners to combat the Japanese kamikaze flyers. Glen and Ding would be two of them. But first, they were granted two weeks' leave.

"Two weeks, Ding," grinned Glen. "With a travel warrant to wherever we want to go. I say Croydon. How about it? Want to come?"

"Sure. But can you warn your friends we're coming? We shouldn't just drop in on them."

Glen shook his head. "I tried to get in touch with them before but the phone lines are hopeless — if they even have a phone. We won't figure on staying. There must be lots of hotels nearby. And one week is not long enough to see everything there is to see in London, even if the Jerries destroyed half of it. For the second week I want to go up to Scotland where my dad came from."

Ding nodded. "Okay. And I guess it's possible your pal may be home on leave."

"Yeah," grinned Glen. "Not to mention his sisters, eh?"

Dressed in their issue blues, with their dress "tiddley" uniforms safely stowed in their duffel bags, Glen and Ding could have been mistaken for a Royal Navy rating, except for the HMCS tally on their caps and "Canada" on their shoulders.

They took the train in to Glasgow, made their way to St.

Enoch's station and settled to await the departure of the 9:27 for London. While waiting at the station they noticed a newspaper headline: "PILOTLESS WARPLANES RAID BRITAIN."

And there was a subheading. Something about "great speed, bright lights and smoke trail" and then "attacks may continue."

"Sounds weird," commented Ding. "Must be remote control. Very expensive proposition for the Jerries. Probably won't amount to much." And they thought no more about it.

The 9:27 left St. Enoch's in Glasgow and travelled overnight to London. It slid so effortlessly out of the station that they were scarcely aware it had started. There was none of the abrupt jerk and jolt they associated with the Canadian trains. And they chuckled at the high, piercing whistle from the comparatively tiny engine, so unlike the mournful, heart-tugging call of the CPR or the CNR. The train gathered speed and the city rapidly dropped behind, street by street, the wheels clickety-clacking over the joints in the track.

Into the black night it went without so much as a lantern to show the way. Only the occasional signal light showed a red or green eye for a few minutes. Every town and village was blacked out. Only the sudden change in the thundering noise of the wheels on the tracks indicated now and then that they were travelling though a tunnel. It would have lulled them to sleep if they could have stretched out.

They were crammed into a compartment that could have seated eight in a degree of comfort, but when the eleventh tried to squeeze in they both gave up and staked out claims to the floor in the corridor, their duffel bags for pillows and their Burberrys for blankets. They were soon joined by others, until the conductor had difficulty threading his way among the supine bodies as he went about the task of collecting tickets.

Daylight roused them as the train hurried through Watford, then Harrow, through busy rail yards where trains from various directions converged on their final run to London. Here they began to see the destruction that had rained on the city from the skies, but not enough to prepare them for the devastation in the city's centre. St. Paul's Cathedral still stood. Bombs had damaged one wing, but the dome was unscathed, a symbol of the unconquerable spirit of a resilient nation. All around it, the city lay in ruins.

Already, however, there were signs of revitalization. Rubble was being cleared from the streets, some damaged walls brought down, others strengthened, while buses threaded their way through the debris. Firemen and ambulances stood by as searchers combed through stricken buildings, and members of the bomb squads in their padded suits waited for the discovery of unexploded bombs.

Glen and Ding stayed overnight at the Canadian Forces hostel on Russell Square, where the damage was minimal. The next day they took the underground to the station where they would catch a train to Croydon. The underground station platforms were home to hundreds of bombed-out people with no other place to call home. They greeted the two Canadian sailors cheerfully. "Thumbs up, boys! It'll soon be over now. It's the Jerries' turn to catch hell now."

The Jerries were catching hell as Allied bombers thundered their way to the continent with their bellies full of high explosive.

But the Britons' ordeal was not yet over.

Chapter Two

COMPARED TO THE CITY centre, Croydon had gotten off lightly during the Battle of Britain. The vicinity of the airfield was battered but there appeared to be little damage in the suburbs, as Glen and Ding discovered as they searched for Waltham Street.

"Number eighteen Waltham?" The Bobby in his blue helmet nodded cheerfully. "Waltham's two — no, three blocks that way. Number eighteen will be to your left when you reach it. Maybe three blocks again. You can't miss it."

The boys *could* miss it, and did so, but not for long. The policeman's directions were not far out. They paused on the opposite side of the street and looked at the home of the Barclays. It was a neat two-storey with a red-tiled roof and bay windows. A garden thick with flowers almost overgrew the walk that led to the front door.

"D'you think they'll recognize you?" wondered Ding.

"Jack would if he were home but I doubt if he is. I don't know about the rest of them. They'll have seen my picture, but of course they won't be expecting me, so probably not. Anyway there's only one way to find out. Let's go."

There was a knocker on the door in the shape of a lion's head. Glen raised it, let it fall, twice. It was only a moment or two before they heard someone inside approaching the door, then they were greeted by an enquiring face, framed by dark hair with just a touch of grey and highlighted by lively blue eyes.

"Good morning. May I help you?"

Glen hesitated. "Mrs. Barclay? I don't suppose you recognize me . . ."

"Wait a minute!" For a moment her face mirrored her struggle with memory. "Of course. You must be Jack's friend! I knew I should know you but I couldn't think how until I saw the 'Canada' flash. Glen, isn't it? Jack will be so disappointed. He's not here, of course. But please, come on in, both of you. This is such a nice surprise. I'm alone at the moment. Steve, my husband, is at work and the family's all left home — the war, you know. But we can't complain. It's the war that has brought you here. And you might have a chance to meet us all before it's over. So you're Glen. I got that right, didn't I? And your friend? I haven't given you a chance to introduce him."

"This is Ding Bell, my winger from the same ship. Sorry. That's what we call him." They were following Mrs. Barclay into a living room where she indicated a chesterfield and comfortable chairs. "What's your *real* name, Ding?" whispered Glen. "I forget."

"If I remember correctly," said Ding seriously, "it's Arthur. But I wouldn't know who you were talking to if you called me that."

"Never mind," said Mrs. Barclay cheerily. "Ding it is. Now, can I get you a nice cup of tea? Then we'll talk. Or do you prefer coffee — if we have any. I suppose you know by now we English survive on our tea. I'm sure we can thank you navy chaps that we were never without our cup of tea."

"Tea would be great, thank you," Glen assured her, giving Ding a warning glance. "Please don't go to any trouble."

"Trouble! It's no trouble at all. A real pleasure." She indicated the mantel above the fireplace. "You will be interested in these pictures. There's the latest of Jack, with his wings, and the girls in their uniforms. I'll just be a few minutes."

"So he's a sergeant air gunner." The familiar face grinned at him posing, so as to display a single air gunner's wing and sergeant's stripes. "He won't want to associate with us lowly seamen any more."

Mrs. Barclay laughed. "You know Jack better than that,"

she called out. She was only steps away, arranging cups and saucers in the kitchen.

"Where is he now? Does he get home often?"

"I don't know where he is. He can't tell me, of course. These restrictions, you know. He could be at the nearest bomber station or up in Scotland for all I know. He's been on bombing trips to the continent. That much I do know. He hasn't been home since he got his wings and I have no idea when we'll see him again."

"That's rough," said Glen, feeling rather helpless.

"That's the way it is with parents in wartime. At least he's much nearer to us than you are to your mum and dad."

Glen suddenly felt guilty. He rarely thought about how his absence might affect his own parents. He had lifted another picture from the mantel and held it so he and Ding could both look at it. Ding whistled a low, appreciative whistle and nudged Glen. "Wow!" He whispered. Glen grinned.

The two girls were there, one with blond hair curling around the rim of her air force cap. Wide eyes and a small chin gave her face a heart shape. The other was dark, like her mother, her straight nose and smiling mouth in perfect symmetry. She didn't appear to be in any uniform.

"That's Heather in the air force, isn't it? What is Susan doing?"

"I'll tell you about them in a minute. They're twins, you know." Mrs. Barclay came in bearing a tray with a teapot, cups and saucers and a tray of biscuits.

"Obviously not identical," observed Ding.

She laughed. "Definitely not identical. They are very different in almost every way. Heather couldn't wait to join the air force. She's into radar, stationed on the coast somewhere. Susan? Not interested in any of that. She has always loved animals and the countryside. So when the chance to join the land army came up she jumped at it."

"Land army? What's that?"

"That's where girls volunteer to work on farms so as to free the young farmers to join the forces. Susan is working on a farm in Cornwall, shepherding sheep, plowing behind a team of horses — not much petrol for the tractor — feeding the chickens, mucking out the stables — she loves it." Mrs. Barclay spread a snowy cloth over a low table, and then set out the cups and saucers and linen napkins, and a china milk and sugar set. "This is such a nice surprise." She began to pour tea into the three cups. "Please help yourselves to the milk and sugar and biscuits."

She watched anxiously as the two boys did so. "You're not taking sugar. We may not get much what with the rationing, but we use very little ourselves and I assure you we have enough."

"That's okay," Glen assured her. "Neither of us takes sugar. Is Mr. Barclay working shifts?"

"Yes. He's foreman in the paint factory. I suppose Jack has told you that. He should be home at nine this evening. He'll be surprised to see you. And delighted. He's also an air raid warden, you know, but he hasn't been very busy in that capacity since the invasion. The German air force is too busy defending their homeland now to send their bombers over here. They're catching it now, the Germans. Day and night. It must be terrible. It was bad enough for us, but it will be worse for them. I feel sorry for them."

"For the Jerries?"

"Yes. Oh, not for Hitler and his Nazis. But for all the innocent mothers and children. *They* have done nothing to deserve this."

"Was it bad here during the Blitz? We saw what happened to London. That must have been terrible."

"Not nearly as bad for us, of course. Mostly the bombers flew right over Croydon on their way to the city centre. Still, we got our share. Dumped bomb loads, crashing planes and so on. We spent many a night in our shelter. We have our own in the back yard, you know. Now, what about you two? You are on leave? From a ship? Where is your ship docked?"

"Actually," said Glen, "it's called Survivor's Leave. Our ship's on the bottom of the North Sea thanks to storm damage and an explosion. But we were lucky. Not a single life lost. So we have two weeks before reporting back. And my first thought was to look up Jack and the family. We didn't expect Jack would be here but hoped to meet the rest of you."

"I'm so glad you came, and Steve will be too. He's not been happy working while others are fighting. Of course he was in the last one — wounded at Ypres — so they wouldn't take him anyway. And people may not think so but the paint factory is a vital industry, though not as obviously as a tank or airplane factory or munitions, or shipyards, of course. They all — planes, tanks, ships and everything else — need paint. Camouflage paint is just one of their specialties."

Glen grinned. "We know all about paint, don't we, Ding. Matelots like us are always painting the ship when the Buffer can't think of anything else to keep us busy. The *Loch Lyon*, our ship, was painted a beautiful two-tone blue and grey. As you say, camouflage."

"Well, do you think you could stay with us for a day or two, or even longer? We have two empty rooms, and there's the shelter as well. That's quite comfortable. So there's lots of room. And there's a good chance Jack will telephone within the next day or so, and you could talk to him."

"Wow! That's very good of you. Yes, I think that would be fine, wouldn't it, Ding? A couple of days anyway. The only thing I want to do before reporting back to base is to go up to the north of Scotland to find the place my granddad came from. I think I'm named after it. A valley actually called Glen Cassley. But your air raid shelter sounds like a fun place to stay."

"Very well, if you would like. After your tea we will go out and look at it."

The air raid shelter was a corrugated iron hut crouching low in the shadows as if burrowing into the ground for safety.

Two steps led down to the doorway, hidden behind blackout curtains. It was furnished, if only in an emergency fashion. There were several chairs that had evidently seen better days but could still offer some degree of comfort. Several camp beds were folded away but a pile of bedding indicated that they could be put to use at a moment's notice. There was a spirit stove in the corner on an open cupboard that housed numerous cups, plates and utensils. Several coal oil lamps apparently provided light when needed, and a radio could keep them informed.

"This is great. Right, Ding? Yes, we'd like to stay here. It's very kind of you."

"It's up to you," said Mrs. Barclay. "We have two empty bedrooms in the house, but this can be quite comfortable if you like." She indicated overhead. "The fan brings in fresh air if it gets stuffy, or you can leave the door open as long as the curtains are in place. Now come into the house and make yourselves at home. Tea will be at six and you must stay in until Steve comes home. He will want to meet you."

Chapter Three

STEVEN BARCLAY ARRIVED home shortly after nine o'clock. He was a big, competent looking man with deep set eyes, a square jaw and a friendly look. He greeted the two boys with delight.

"This is wonderful. Jack will be so disappointed. So will the girls. I think they would be just as happy to meet you as Jack would. As Ruth said, if you can stay for a few days there is a good chance that one or two of them — or all three — will call, and you will have a chance to talk to them. Now, I'm on duty tonight. Warden, you know. I expect it will be a quiet night. No bombers have come over for the last two weeks. My post is on Warminster Road and that will take me right past the Control Centre. Would you like to come along and see how we operate?"

"Very much. Right, Ding? You're sure we won't be in the way?"

He chuckled. "Don't worry. If you're in the way we'll tell you. But as I said, it will be a quiet night."

It was only a short walk to the Control Centre. It was heavily sandbagged, partially underground. Behind black-out curtains several people were at their posts, including three women at a switchboard, their tin hats and gas masks hanging within arm's reach. Here those in control received reports of "incidents" from the various wardens placed strategically around the borough. It was common for many reports to come in at once as a fleet of aircraft dropped their bombs. The calls were analyzed and prioritized and then relayed to the fire department, the police, the ambulances and first aid depots, rescue parties and the bomb squads.

"It can be hectic at times," said Steve. "We have to ask where is the greatest need, the greatest danger, the worst fire, the most casualties? Thank God, it seems to be over."

"Nothing doing tonight, Steve," a uniformed man reported.

"That's good news, Chief. I'd like you to meet two friends of Jack's from Canada. Glen and — er — Ding. Their ship got a sub but went down herself so they're on Survivor's Leave."

"Congratulations. What happened?"

"It was storm damage to our bottom plates that did it.

Our depth charge blew up a torpedo before it hit us but the explosion was too much for our weakened bottom plates and she sank. But there was no loss of life."

"That's good news. We can always replace ships. Too bad you're missing Jack. Any news from him, Steve?"

"Nothing new. He's in bombers somewhere."

"Aye, that's right. It's Jerry's turn to be on the receiving end. Think it's all over for us, Steve? Have you heard anything about this new invention — the flying bomb?"

"Just what's in the papers, something about one coming down in Kent and killing a pig or something. We'll worry about them when and if they ever materialize. Well, boys, it's time I was relieving my opposite number. See you, Chief. Good luck. Come, lads."

The city was blacked out, but there was a full moon riding high, with only an occasional cloud drifting across its face, so the houses on both sides of the street were clearly distinguishable, casting bulky shadows. It was a residential district. Behind the blackout curtains most families were listening to the late news or were already in bed. In most of them there were pictures of young men and women in uniform, sons and daughters, or fathers and even mothers, serving their country in outposts around the world. Many of them would not return.

Steve Barclay, with the two boys, was walking towards his post, when they heard it.

First it was a distant throbbing mutter like a motorcycle

revving its engine; then it came closer until it was a deep-throated roar, somewhere in the moonlit sky.

"What's that?" wondered Ding. "It doesn't sound like any aircraft I've ever heard."

"That's right. It's . . . *Look!*" Steve pointed.

There was an object, like an oddly shaped airplane, black against the moonlight, streaking across the sky, with a tail of flame and smoke.

"It's a plane. On fire!"

"No! There's no plane shaped like that!" Steve's voice was tight. "It must be one of Jerry's new bombs — remote control. No crew aboard."

They had stopped and were staring upward, watching it. Suddenly the flame cut out. For just a second or two the roar continued then stopped abruptly. The black object wavered, then it was falling, hurtling out of the sky.

"Down!" yelled Steve. "Flat! Cover your heads. It's a bomb."

Glen flung himself flat on the road, aware that the other two did the same. For a moment, an eternity, there was nothing. Then there was a blinding flash, a blast of wind that clutched at his clothes and that would have blown him across the street if he had been standing. An ear-shattering explosion. Then debris was raining down on him. He buried his head in his arms. With thuds and crumps, things fell on him, pummelling his body. Something hit him on the legs, then his head, and for a time he lost consciousness, then he came to again and stirred. Slowly he looked up.

All around was chaos. He could hear walls crumbling, people screaming, shouting, running. The very street beneath him trembled with the crash of falling timbers. And almost at once the sound of sirens, not far away, coming quickly.

"Get back!" someone was shouting. "I know there's someone in there. They'll have to wait. That wall's going to give way any minute. No use getting killed. You, there, give me a hand with this beam. *Watch it!*" More sounds of walls falling, debris settling, muffled cries for help.

He had to do what he could. Glen struggled to turn and sit up, pushing a beam from across his legs. It hurt but he knew it wasn't serious. The pain in his arm — he realized there was blood running down it. Glass, he thought. There was a lot of it lying around. He looked for Ding and Mr. Barclay. Steve was bending over Ding, then turned and glanced at Glen. There was blood on his face, he was covered in white plaster dust. He didn't seem to notice. "Your pal's been hit on the head but he's breathing. He'll be taken to First Aid. How about you? Are you okay?"

"Yes. I'm fine." He was staring around in disbelief at the damage. The bomb had landed between two rows of four houses each that stood back to back. All eight were nothing but piles of rubble and a few sagging walls, one of which, even as he stared, teetered and fell, raising a choking cloud of dust. The houses beyond still stood but had been blasted open to the skies.

Mr. Barclay reached out to help Glen to his feet.

"We'll need all the help we can get. There's people trapped in those houses." He played his flashlight over Glen and noticed the blood on his hand. "We'll take care of that later. Right now there's a woman and baby in there somewhere." He motioned to what had been the end house. "Luckily there's no fire. Not yet anyway. I know her. She must be in there somewhere. Be careful, Glen. Don't move anything without being told."

Already men were converging on the scene. One man was taking charge. "Hello, Steve. This is the Johnsons' home, right? You know them? All right, I'll leave you to it. You need some help? Ah, I see you have some. Fine." He turned. "This way, men. There's someone under that pile there. I can hear them. Take care now . . . "

Glen was aware of an organized effort to help, the men going about their grim task quickly and efficiently. They had trained for this. An ambulance was picking its way through the rubble littering the street, followed by a fire engine. There was no sign of fire, thank God, but the firemen were running to help with axes and jacks. And as if by magic, an army truck appeared and soldiers were jumping down, eager to help.

"This way, Glen. Careful, now." Steve was pulling aside beams and lath, stopping every now and then to listen. "I don't hear anyone, but she must be here. Her man's away in Burma. Give me a hand with this."

With infinite care they moved a heavy beam, pushed aside litter. The upper floor had fallen in on top of the lower. A toilet was hanging grotesquely in mid-air on its pipe. A bath was on its back, short legs stuck up in the air.

"She slept downstairs. So she's under all this somewhere. There's a good chance she'll be alive. Ah, that's better." Someone had produced a powerful light and turned it on the remains of the Johnson house. "I'll . . . *Listen!*"

They both heard it. A tiny cry, a moment's silence, then an unmistakable wail. "The baby!" Steve grinned. "Right about there. I hope the mother's okay. Here, Glen."

Carefully, they began to move aside debris. Soon they came to recognizable furnishings: a table, shattered chairs, a bed on end bent almost double. And there was a baby's crib. Two beams were resting across it. They had formed a make-shift shelter. The cry came from under there.

"That's the baby. With any luck the mother too . . . "

Glen brushed plaster dust impatiently from his eyes, leaving a smear of blood. There seemed to be glass everywhere. You had to ignore it. The baby, maybe the mother, that's all that mattered.

"This way. Help me move this, lad." Mr. Barclay was struggling with a beam. "If we can move it just a little, I think we can get in underneath."

With rubble moving beneath his feet, threatening to upset him, Glen heaved on the beam, raising it a little but noticed another move as if about to collapse. He stopped. "I think that will do, Mr. Barclay. I could crawl in there and reach the baby."

"Let me see." Steve was beside him. "There's not much room."

"Not for you," agreed Glen. "You're too big. But I can do it."

Mr. Barclay hesitated only a moment. "Right. We can't lose any time. If I lever up on this. No. Wait just a minute. Here's Johnny with some gloves. You'll need them for the glass. And my torch."

Glen nodded. He pulled on a pair of thick gloves, gratefully aware that they would save his hands from further cuts, clutched the flashlight and edged carefully into the gap between the beams.

The beam rested on a crib rail preventing any heavy debris from falling into it. The baby lay there, covered with dust and bits of plaster but awake and apparently unhurt. He — or was it she? — watched Glen with big, questioning eyes. Glen grinned.

"You're okay," he said, reassuringly. "We'll have you out in a minute. I hope." He added the last two words in a whisper to himself. He felt around to find the pin that held the rail up. It was there. He could release it if he could take the weight of the beam off it. Otherwise, if he lowered it, the beam would come down with it, onto the baby. What was he to do?

He tried lifting one of the beams. He could barely move it. And how was he to lift it and at the same time reach the child? But it *had* to be done. He hunkered down until he was under one of the beams, then raised his back. The beam was heavy, biting into his back. He gritted his teeth. Sweat mixed with dust and blood ran into his eyes. He tried to blink it away. He couldn't hope to hold up more than the one beam with his back. The other would go down with the rail, but it would miss the baby. So he could reach the child and lift him, or her, out. But then what? How was he to get out from under the beam? He had to have something to prop it up while he crawled out from under.

"Glen! Are you all right? Can you do it?" Steve was anxious.

"I need something to prop the beam up. If I lower the rail it will come down onto the kid."

"All right. There are jacks. I'll see if there's one available. Hang on."

It was only a few minutes but it seemed an eternity before Steve was pushing a jack into the gap. Glen grabbed it, worked it under the beam, pumped the lever until the jack was taking the weight of the beam. Very carefully he lowered the rail and lifted the baby out, cradling it. He turned slowly to the gap.

"Here he is, Mr. Barclay." He held the child out, felt rather than saw Mr. Barclay take it from him.

"Thanks, Glen. Good job. Any sign of the mother?"

"No. Not that I can see."

"All right. We'll try over this way. Now, can you get that jack back. We'll need it."

"Okay." It took him a long time working in the narrow space, to free the jack without trapping himself under the beams, but he managed it at last and crawled out.

The whole scene seemed to be floodlit now. For the first

time he saw the unbelievable extent of the damage from a single bomb. Mr. Barclay clasped his hand for a moment, then indicated a van nearby. "Take a few minutes for a cup of tea, lad. The Sally Ann is here, as always."

The Salvation Army was indeed there, handing out tea and biscuits to whoever could take a few minutes from their desperate efforts to save lives. Glen accepted a mug of hot Bovril, cupping it in bloody hands. He realized with surprise that they were trembling. One of the girls in the van noticed it.

"You're bleeding, sailor. Is it a cut? Better have it looked at."

"No, thanks. Just from the glass. It's not much." He stopped short. The wail of the air-raid warning rose and fell eerily. Rather late for that, he thought. Then a new sound came to them, a throbbing roar that increased until it became deafening. Everyone looked skyward.

"Holy smoke!" muttered Glen in awe.

There were more of them, lots more, streaking across the sky, like a gaggle of fast-moving geese, each trailing a tail of flame and smoke. And one by one the motors cut out and the bombs wavered, then fell. All around were deafening explosions, brilliant, dazzling flares like lingering lightning. Another bomb fell only a block away, knocking men to their knees, riddling them with dust and glass and splinters, scarring faces, blinding them. And there was fire now, red tongues leaping and reaching eagerly for what was little more than match wood.

"Come, Glen." Mr. Barclay touched Glen's shoulder. "One thing at a time. We can't fight all the bombs. There's others to take care of them. I think we've located Mrs. Johnson under there." He pointed. "We found her neighbour. He says she was in the kitchen just a few minutes before the bomb hit so she's likely under that lot."

Glen turned his back on the mad scene around him, shutting out everything but this one pile of rubble and wood. A man had joined them, a little man dressed in a torn bathrobe, a dazed look on his face.

"Mr. Lucas." Steve had recognized him. "Glad to see you're okay. Your wife . . . ?"

"They've taken her. She's gone, Mr. Barclay." Tears filled his eyes. He blinked them away.

"You mean . . . Oh gosh, Mr. Lucas I'm so sorry. Why don't you . . . The medics will take you to her."

"No no, Mr. Barclay. There's nothing I can do for her now. But I can help others. That's what she would have wanted. Mrs. Johnson is under this somewhere?"

"Yes." For a moment Steve clutched the little man's hand. "Yes. We think she must be."

"Then I can help." Mr. Lucas was in shock. He began to pull debris aside, roughly, unthinking, endangering the stability of the mass of litter. As if he had to be doing something, anything. Steve touched him gently on the arm. "Give me a hand with this, Mr. Lucas."

He shone his light on a heavy beam lying crosswise. "Glen will look for Mrs. Johnson under there while we clear some of this rubbish."

Glen found the baby's mother, her arms around her head,

giving her a little breathing space. She was unconscious, but alive. He began to remove some of the rubble imprisoning her, then stopped, catching his breath. Her legs were bent at an impossible angle, one at least crushed and bloody.

"Mr. Barclay," he called, his voice croaking. "I found her. She's alive, but I don't think *we* can move her. Her legs . . . "

She stirred, her eyes opened. Pain-filled eyes. "My baby." she whispered. "My baby . . . "

"Your baby is fine," Glen assured her, leaning close. "He's being taken care of and you will be soon." But she had relapsed into unconsciousness.

Steve was there beside him. "You're right. We'll have to wait for a doctor and ambulance crew to move her. Just make sure nothing else falls onto her."

It seemed like hours before a doctor arrived, as more explosions erupted all around, interrupting the screams of sirens, the shouts of searchers, the crackle of fire. Glen kept an eye on the woman, but he was beginning to feel the effects of the blast and his struggle to move the beams. He noticed blood on his hand when he tried to brush the sweat from his face. One arm seemed to be on fire, and now and then the whole scene seemed to float in the air, turn lazily upside down before settling back where it should be.

He was relieved when three men arrived, and a doctor crouched down beside him. Glen gestured to the woman still lying in the rubble.

"All right, young fellow. Don't worry. We'll take care of

the lady." He looked for a moment at Glen, then turned and called out.

"Steve Barclay? Your lad here. He could do with some medical attention himself. See he gets it, will you."

"Yes, doctor. He's done a great job. Now it's his turn."

"I'm okay — "

Steve interrupted him. "No, Glen. The doctor's right. We have to look after ourselves as well as others. I'll get someone to take you home — to my place. Reassure Ruth, my wife, that I'm all right. She must be wondering. That is if *she's* all right. One of those bombs must have hit not far from the house. Anyway, she'll look after your cuts and bruises — she's a nurse, you know."

"It's okay. I can get there on my own. I know the way, Mr. Barclay."

Steve hesitated, then nodded. "All right. Take care . . . "

Chapter Four

"PENRAVEN." THE MAN who spoke was heavy set with a broad face and dark brows over piercing blue eyes. The eyes were regarding the other closely. "Penraven," he repeated. "Does that mean anything to you?"

The younger man frowned in thought, then shook his head. "No, sir. Should it?"

"I was hoping it might. It is the last word spoken by a dying man."

"Oh." The lean, athletic man swallowed. "Who? Not Rogers?"

"Yes, unfortunately. Rogers."

"Damn! How did it happen, sir?"

"Who knows? As you are well aware, he was undercover in the Nazi laboratories. How he ever wormed his way into their confidence we'll never know. Their labs are on an island in the Baltic under tons of concrete, as safe from our bombers as the U-boat pens at Lorient. We're doing the same research, of course, on an island off the west coast of Scotland, working with micro-organisms — germ warfare, they call it." He shuddered. "The Nazis are way ahead of us. They're very close to achieving their goal. Too close. I suspect that Rogers took a chance to warn us about that and was caught. He was only able to get in touch with West by telephone. He was gasping, dying, I guess. He just managed to say that one word and that was it. West got out of there fast; they would no doubt trace the call. He's safe, but that's all he can give us: Penraven."

The younger man turned for a moment and looked silently out over the London traffic, then he turned back. "It sounds like a village, probably in Cornwall. What have you been able to find out?"

"There's no town or village by that name anywhere in the UK. There *is* an estate, and it's in Cornwall, on the coast. There's a manor house and a few acres belonging to Sir Godfrey Trevour. Sir Godfrey's a widower, has two sons, both in the service, one in the Far East, the other in Kent, RAF. A man, a boy and a Land Army girl do the actual work. Everything seems normal and above board. But of course we have to check it out."

"And that's where I come in? Right. Anything else you can tell me?"

The big man shook his head. "The house itself is in poor shape — going downhill ever since the collapse of the tin mining trade. And it's reputed to be haunted. Nothing unusual there."

"No, but it might come in useful. I might develop a sudden interest in the occult."

"That's up to you. Carry on and report as soon as you have something."

"Yes sir." The younger man went out, frowning. The older man stood, in turn, at the window, looking down on the London traffic. He was worried. Penraven! Nothing much to go on . . .

Chapter Five

THE BARCLAYS' HOUSE WAS undamaged but it was in darkness and there was no answer to his knock. He turned to the shelter, pulled aside the blackout curtains and slipped inside. It had been turned into a miniature dressing station, Ruth Barclay presiding. There were several women, at least one man and a number of children having various cuts and bruises attended to. Mrs. Barclay saw him. Her eyes lit up.

"Glen! Steve, is he . . . ?"

"He's fine. Very busy rescuing people. He told me to come. I have — "

"Yes, I can see you need some attention. Your head . . . where's your hat?"

"Holy cow! My hat! I don't know. And my uniform! How'm I going to explain this mess to the Regulating Petty Officer in charge of stores? He'll have a fit."

She laughed. "That's the least of your worries. We can always have that cleaned and pressed and get another cap. But your head needs a bandage and those cuts need cleaning up before they fester. Where's your friend Ding?"

"He was taken to a First Aid post with concussion but it's not serious — or so I was told."

"Right. Sit here. I'll tend to you in a minute. Meantime have a cup of tea."

The tea was good! He was going to become a regular "tea granny," Glen thought. It was just what he needed. He watched Ruth dressing wounds, cheering up frightened children, assuring anxious parents, while all the time there was the sound of shrill sirens, and reverberating explosions so that the ground shook and the shelter trembled. But it would take a direct hit to destroy this building and in that event those inside would never know what hit them.

So all through that desperate night, and for several more days and nights, death and destruction followed Glen and Ding.

The borough of Croydon, which had escaped the worst of the earlier bombing, made up for it now. The flying bombs, known variously as "Buzz-Bombs" and "Doodlebugs" may have been meant for London city itself, but probably through some miscalculations by those releasing them, they fell short, on Croydon and other suburbs that became known as "Doodlebug Alley."

They came at night and they came in broad daylight. You could watch them in the daytime, watch and listen for the telltale signs that the bomb was about to fall, and try to act accordingly. At night it was a different matter. If you weren't fighting fires and rescuing casualties you could either spend the nights in shelters or stay at home and hope for the best. You could lie in bed and listen to the sound of night fighters and gunfire, the whine of the bombs themselves — and then, worst of all, the sudden sound of silence.

Ding was soon released from the First Aid post, none the worse for the experience, and he and Glen endured the bombing for a week, helping whenever possible in any way they could. They were wondering what to do with the remaining week of their Survivor's Leave, when their problem was solved for them. It came in the form of a telephone call.

Ruth Barclay answered the phone. Glen and Ding, resting in the living room, heard her answer it.

"Susan!" they heard her exclaim, pleasure in her voice. "How nice to hear from you . . . Oh yes, dear, we're surviving . . . Yes, Jack and Heather both called . . . worried about us, of course, but we're managing fine. They're both doing very well, but of course they can't tell us anything. Your father is very busy as warden and so am I, tending to cuts and bruises and to the boys — What boys? Oh, haven't I told you? No, I haven't, have I, what with everything. It's Glen Cassley and a friend ... Glen Cassley. Doesn't that name ring a bell? Think . . . That's right. Jack's pen pal from Canada. He's here on leave. Survivor's Leave, they call it. With a friend called Ding ... I don't really know. Something to do with his name, which I believe is Bell. Yes, of course, that must be it. Ding Dong. You're faster on the uptake than I am. They've been here for — it must be a week now — and they've been a big help in the raids. But they'll be leaving in a day or so. They still have a week before reporting back to a base up in Scotland somewhere . . . Where are they going? ... I don't know. I don't think they've decided. Would you like to talk to Glen? Certainly. He's right here. Just a moment."

She poked her head around the corner of the door and beckoned Glen.

"It's Susan — one of the twins, you know. She would like to talk to you."

"Susan?" Which one was she? Of course, the brunette, the one who worked on a farm. He took the phone from her mother.

"Susan? Hi! This is Glen Cassley, Jack's pen pal. How are you?"

"Oh *I'm* fine. We haven't had any doodlebugs bothering us here. Mum said something about Survivor's Leave? Does that mean what I think it means? That you've survived more than buzz bombs?"

"Well, yes, we had a ship sink from under us, but we didn't

even get our feet wet. The buzz bombs have been much more exciting."

"Well, it seems to me you deserve a few days of peace and quiet. Have you any plans for the next week?"

"No, not yet. My dad came from Scotland and I want to look up his birthplace eventually. We'll probably head north . . ."

"Well, before you do, I think I have an idea — "

"You *think* you have?"

"Yes. It hit me so suddenly I haven't had time to think it out. You haven't had a chance to meet Jack, have you?"

"No. He's too busy bombing Germany and shooting down their night fighters."

"Or Heather?"

"No. She's too busy doing whatever it is she does."

"Then we mustn't let you go without meeting at least one of us. How about coming to see me."

"Oh. Well that sounds great, but just where are you, how do we get there and where could we stay?"

"I'm working on a farm. Did Mum tell you that? It's here in Cornwall, overlooking the Atlantic Ocean. You come by train. Mum and Dad will set you on the right train. And when you get here we'll set you up in very comfortable rooms with views to take your breath away, with good farm produce to eat — "

Glen interrupted. "You're sure this is a *farm* you're working on? It sounds like an expensive resort."

"Well, it's not your usual farm," she admitted. "It's an

estate belonging to a wealthy man whose boys are away in the forces. Well, he used to be wealthy, anyway. Every bit of his land, including lawns and tennis courts have been plowed under and seeded, his Rolls Royce has been stored along with a tractor because we can't get petrol for either and we have to use horses. But there's plenty of room in the house. I suppose you might call it a mansion. And the owner, Sir Godfrey Trevour, would like to meet you, I'm sure. He's just mad that he can't be in the forces himself — "

"Did you say *Sir* Godfrey something or other?"

"Yes. He's a baronet. But he's quite human. You'll like him. I'm sure I could get a day or two off to entertain you if you could come. What do you think?"

"Well . . . it sounds great. Yes, I don't see why we couldn't do that. We have another week before reporting back, and I know Ding would agree. We both want to meet you. When? Any particular time?"

"I would suggest right away. It's too late today but how about tomorrow? I'll meet all the trains until I see you. Let me talk to Mum again and we'll arrange it. By the way the place is called Penraven."

Chapter One

THE SOUTHERN RAILWAY train bound for Plymouth pulled out of Waterloo station at nine in the morning. Glen and Ding boarded early to secure window seats opposite each other but they needn't have hurried. Only two more passengers had entered their compartment before the train eased out of the station. An army corporal slipped into the seat by the door to the corridor, acknowledged the two sailors with a brief wave of his hand and settled back with closed eyes. A tall man in civilian clothes, slim, with a shock of wavy blond hair, lifted a travelling bag onto the overhead rack and pulled a copy of the morning paper from his pocket. He glanced briefly at the sailors.

"Morning lads," he said. "Nice day." He sat down and opened his paper.

Glen and Ding watched out the window in silence as the train pulled out of the station into the battered city. Here and there whole streets had been levelled, some with smoke still drifting upward from the latest raid.

"Know something?" murmured Glen. "I feel guilty, leaving the Barclays and the rest of the people of Croydon to battle the doodlebugs while we go off on a holiday where they've never even seen a doodlebug or an enemy bomber."

Ding nodded. "Me too. But hey! We'll soon be going to battle the kamikazes so we'd better make the most of it."

"Yeah. You're right, of course."

They were silent then as the city gradually fell behind and they came to open country. Some time passed, then the man with the paper put it aside with a noncommittal grunt and turned to look at the boys. For the first time he noticed their shoulder flashes.

"Ah. Canada, eh? Good show. You all came through when we needed you — all the empire, I mean. And the Yanks, of course. Headed for Plymouth, I expect? No no." He held up his hand. "Sorry. I'm not supposed to ask such questions, am I? Maybe I'm a Nazi spy for all you know." He grimaced. "'Loose lips sink ships,' eh? Lots of truth in that, I expect."

Glen laughed. "In this case there's no harm in your knowing the truth. We're on leave and we're *not* going to Plymouth. Beyond Plymouth, actually. Well into Cornwall."

"Ah. That's interesting. So am I, as a matter of fact. I'm a writer doing a book on Cornwall manor houses. Looking for some interesting historic anecdotes, in particular. Ghosts, of course. I understand every respectable Cornish manor house has its resident ghost — at least one, that comes and goes. Whereabouts are you headed, may I ask?"

"A village called Polgarth. Wherever that is."

"Polgarth? Wait a minute I'm sure that name . . . " He drew a notebook from his pocket and flipped through some pages. "Yes. Thought so. Here it is. Apparently there's an interesting manor house nearby. Named — let's see — Penraven."

"You're kidding!" Glen and Ding exchanged glances. "That's where we're going. Penraven!"

"Are you really! Now that's a coincidence. I see the family name is Trevour. May I ask . . . do you know the family?"

"No. We just know the Land Army girl working there on the farm. Her brother is a friend of mine, has been for years. As a pen pal, that is. He's away off somewhere in the air force so we can't go to see him but his sister has got permission for us to stay at Penraven for a few days."

"Well, well. We'll be travelling companions for some time then. I haven't any set schedule so I might as well start off at Polgarth. That is, if there's such a thing as a hotel there, or a decent pub. By the way, I'm Jim Peters." He held out a hand to each of them. They introduced themselves. "Glen Cassley? Right. And Ding? Bell! Of course. I get the connection."

He looked past them out the window. The train had slowed to a crawl. "This will be the village of Hook, I expect . . . "

There was no warning. Not this time. They had no glimpse of a flying machine trailing a plume of fire. They heard no whistle of a bomb hurtling from the sky. Perhaps that was because they were enclosed, in the train coach.

It all happened in a moment yet it seemed to go on forever. The rails, several sets of them between the train and the station, suddenly rose bodily into the air, turning, twisting into fantastic shapes like pretzels. The station house disintegrated, slowly, into a pile of smoking rubble. The trees that lined the walk to the station were stripped of their branches and leaves in one startling moment and left standing there, naked and shivering. A man who had emerged from the station rose abruptly into the air as if he had suddenly discovered the art of flying, arms flailing. He disappeared, somewhere beyond the train.

All this Glen and Ding saw, through glass that shattered and smacked them in the face, cutting their cheeks, bloodying their heads, while a blow like a fist smacked into the train and tipped it up so they were sliding helplessly into the other passengers.

They didn't see it until later, but there was a smoking black crater where the tracks had been.

"No doodlebug did *that*." They were standing by the crater, staring into it. Ding had a bandage covering five stitches in his forehead, Glen had a plaster covering a gash on his cheek but once the blood had been washed away they discovered that they had no serious injuries to worry about. They stood now, waiting for a bus to arrive and carry them on their way. It was Jim Peters who spoke. "You've seen what doodlebugs do, haven't you? Did you ever see a hole like that?"

"No. Never. What does it mean? A new weapon of some sort?"

"The bomb must have fallen from a tremendous height. I suspect it's what the Jerries have been predicting for years, and Churchill warned us would come sooner or later. A rocket bomb. Fired into the stratosphere where no airplanes or gunfire can reach it. Then released by remote control. Fantastic. But too late to do them — the Jerries — any good."

"But why *here*, for heaven's sake. A few tracks gone, one building destroyed, some trees stripped and what? Two killed and a few casualties? Hardly worth the price, surely?"

"Oh no doubt this wasn't the target. There's always flaws to overcome in new weapons. Something went wrong with the direction finder or something, I suppose. They'll be a lot more accurate with the next ones. You can count on that."

"Too little, too late, as far as they're concerned, I guess. They will kill a lot of people though. You won't know they're coming till they hit. Not like the doodlebugs. At least you had a chance with them."

"Know what?" said Ding. "These things aren't going to worry people at all. Since you won't know till it's too late, what's the use of worrying?"

"I think you're absolutely right," nodded Jim Peters. "One more weapon too late. What do you suppose they will come up with next?"

Glen shook his head. "They're running out of time. I bet this was their last kick at the can."

Jim looked at him and shook his head, just a fraction. "I wouldn't count on that."

Chapter Two

THE TRAIN RUNNING WEST from the shattered city of Plymouth skirted the lonely wastes of Bodmin Moor, where sudden tors rose from bare rock fields, where tendrils of mist clung to the ground and wound like wraiths around ancient standing stones.

Here and there, in the moor and beyond as they entered more fertile country, they saw what looked like historic ruins rearing up out of the landscape.

Glen pointed them out. "What are those? Ancient castles? They look like crumbling keeps. Am I right?"

"No. Not those. There are lots of castle ruins in Cornwall, of course," explained Jim Peters. "Like Tintagel. Ever heard of that? The legend of King Arthur? Everyone has heard of him, I suppose. But those things you see are actually engine houses and chimney stacks marking old mine entrances. Tin, copper and zinc. Some of them — the mines, I mean — are hundreds of feet deep. Abandoned for many years now. If you hear someone mention "Cornish castles" he's probably talking about those things rather than real castles. You'll see more of those all the way to the coast. It was Cornwall's main industry until the bottom fell out of the trade."

There *were* more of them, here and there, as the train moved on until it dropped the three of them off at a tiny wayside station to await yet another train to take them on the spur line to the village of Polgarth. This one, when it eventually arrived, was made up of a single coach, the no-corridor type pulled by a tank engine that puffed and poured out smothering clouds of smoke and steam, as it gallantly crossed more rain-washed moorland and gently rolling hills.

Twenty minutes or so later, the train pulled into a tiny station with a snort and a bump. A conductor appeared from somewhere, running along beside the train as it slowed.

"This is it, gents. Polgarth Station."

"So here we go," said Jim Peters cheerfully. "I'll look for a hotel. How about you two? Do you know how to get to Penraven?"

"That'll be no problem. Susan's meeting us. At least I hope she is. We were supposed to get here yesterday but that bomb back there at — what was it — Hoot? Anyway, it meant we're a day late."

"It's okay." Ding was leaning out the door as the train came to a shuddering stop. "Bet you anything that's Susan there, on the platform."

"I think you're right," nodded Jim. "I'll go and look for accommodation and very possibly see you later on."

"No. Just a minute. Susan may be able to direct you. I'll introduce you."

A few moments later Glen was aware of dark, wavy hair, startling blue eyes, a friendly smile and then a warm hand-shake — and, barely audible, Ding's "*Wow!*"

"You're Glen," Susan Barclay was saying. "I recognize you from Jack's picture." She turned to Ding. "And you must be Mr. Bell."

"No, you got that wrong. I'm just Ding — unless you want to be formal. In that case I'm Mr. Dong."

She laughed, a catchy laugh. "Right. You're Ding. I'm so glad to see you both. But I was expecting you yesterday. And you look as if you've been in the wars. What happened?"

When Glen explained, she whistled. "Thank God you're safe. And you've come to the right place. You won't have to worry about any enemy weapons here. Did you have a good trip otherwise?"

"Very good. Except maybe that last bit . . . "

She laughed. "That would be our spur line. It only serves three stations, none of them very important as far as the war effort goes, so we're left with whatever rolling stock no one else wants. Still, it got you here. That's what's important. Sorry I'm not dressed for the occasion." She was wearing a thick roll-neck sweater, knee breeches and rubber boots. "I've just come from the hay mow, as you can see." She plucked some wisps of hay from her sweater. "Is that all your luggage?" She indicated the bag each was carrying. "Fine. Pre-war you would have been met by a chauffeur-driven Rolls, but as I told you we are short of petrol, so we have to travel by horse and cart. Still, we don't have far to go. About three miles."

"Just a moment," broke in Glen. "There's a man here — a fellow passenger who's looking for somewhere to stay for a few days. A hotel or pub. This is Jim Peters."

"Hello Jim." She held out a hand to him. "We don't have a hotel here in Polgarth but there is a pub of course. I hear it's very comfortable, though I've never had to stay there myself. It's just down the street at the corner." She pointed.

"Ah. I see it. The Grey Gull. Thanks very much, Miss. Who knows, I may meet *you* again soon. I'm interested in Penraven. The boys will explain . . . "

She looked after him as he swung down the street. "What will you explain?"

"Just that he's writing a book about Cornwall manor houses and will likely start with Penraven."

"Oh. I see. Well, I suppose Penraven may be what he's looking for." She turned to where a heavy farm horse, hitched to a two-wheeled cart, was tethered to a rail. "This is Charlie." She patted the horse's long nose. "Charlie, meet Glen and Ding. Charlie's never in a hurry," she explained, "so we won't be either. There's hay in the body of the cart but I think there's room for all three of us on the seat if we squeeze together."

The boys were quite willing to squeeze together, with Susan between them.

She picked up the reins, then, before starting out, she indicated the village. "This is Polgarth, where we do our shopping for Penraven." There were several shops, a square-towered church, and a number of houses, each with its small garden overflowing with flowers. "There's a dance in the church hall every Wednesday evening, especially for servicemen. That's tonight, in case you've lost track of time. Would you like to come in for that?"

"Yeah. That sounds like fun," said Ding. "Right, Glen?"

"Sure."

"Great. We'll do that. So what is your impression of Cornwall?" she asked.

"Parts of it are very bleak," said Glen. "That would be the moor, I guess. What is it? Bodmin, I think the man said."

"Right, Bodmin Moor. Yes, that's certainly bleak, but it can be beautiful, too, at times. The wild flowers, the sun painting the rock with lots of colours. But we're beyond the moors here. As you can see."

They were into farmland with sheep and cattle grazing in fields bounded by stone dykes, and gently rolling green hills. And there was another ancient-looking ruin stark against the sky.

Ding pointed it out. "I see those things aren't just on the moors," he said.

"You mean the Cornwall castles? No, they're everywhere. There's one just beyond Penraven. That's where the Penraven money came from, tin mining. That and smuggling." She chuckled. "But the bottom fell out of the tin markets so it's been closed down for many years."

"What was that about smuggling?" asked Ding, intrigued.

"Penraven's on the clifftop and the cliff itself is riddled with caves. Carved out by the ocean, of course. The restless, pounding ocean. The cliffs are high, hundreds of feet, and the spray from the surf still reaches above them. The caves are hard to get to, especially by land, which made them an ideal spot for smugglers to hide their contraband in. This was in the old days when they smuggled tobacco and spirits and silks and anything that had to be imported. Anything that otherwise you would have to pay taxes on. It was very lucrative, and pretty safe.

"Sir Godfrey's grandfather was in the thick of it, or so it was generally believed, but he was never caught. He seems to have been a bit of a rogue, but his son was a member of parliament and made the family name respectable. Now the present Sir Godfrey lives in the big house, or part of it. It's pretty run down. Mostly, he travels and plays at farming. When the war came along every bit of arable land had to be cultivated to feed the nation. He had to take up farming seriously. In other words, he had to hire more people to do it for him. Me included. And I'm enjoying it very much."

The cart topped a long, gentle rise and suddenly a vista opened out before them. Green fields sloped upwards away from them and at the far edge stood a manor house. It was a huge mansion, almost a castle, thought Glen, several wings three storeys high, with crow-stepped gables and tall chimneys. A curved, hedge-lined driveway led to an impressive pillared entrance. Beyond the building there seemed to be nothing but the sky. Apparently it stood close to the edge of a cliff.

"Wow!" said Glen. "That's some house." He remembered what Jim Peters had said about Cornwall mansions.

"Is there a ghost connected with Penraven?" he asked.

Susan looked at him in surprise. "Why? Have you heard something?"

"Jim Peters said every respectable manor house has a resident ghost."

She laughed. "He may be right, at that. The house *is* reputed to be haunted though I've never seen any sign of it. Of course any ghost would stick to the old parts of the house, and I'm more or less restricted to the servants' quarters. As you will be, too, as my guests."

The main road led to the front of the house but she steered the horse off onto a rough track that led to the outbuildings. The door to one of the barns opened and a man came to meet them, a squat, square man with black hair growing low on his forehead.

"Ah, Susan. I see you met your friends." He came up to the cart with an extended hand. "I'm Jake."

"Hi, Jake. I'm Glen and this is Ding. Pleased to meet you."

"Welcome to Penraven. The boy and I will take care of everything now, Susan. You look after your two friends."

"Thanks, Jake. I appreciate that. Is Sir Godfrey in, do you know?"

"Far as I know, yes. He'll likely be taking his nap about now. Maybe best you wait awhile before introducing your guests."

"I think you're right. Well, come in, lads, to meet the staff."

She led the way to a side door of the house, opened it, pushed through the blackout curtains, and called out.

"Hello, Mr. Crane! Martha! Lucy! Mrs. Crane!" As they waited beside her for a few moments, she explained. "Mr. Crane is the butler, his wife is the housekeeper, Martha is the cook and Lucy Fenwick the maid. There are only the four living in this part of the house, the servants' quarters, besides myself. There used to be eight or nine. It takes quite a few to run a place this size but the rest are day help. That's why there is room for you."

"How about Jake, and the boy he mentioned?"

"The farm hands. They live over the garage. Ah, here's Mr. Crane."

Glen didn't know what to expect of a butler, so he was not surprised when the man appeared, a tall almost elegant man, dressed impeccably in tails. He had a pale, expressionless face, that is, until he saw Susan, and then a smile of pleasure broke out.

"Ah, Miss Barclay. These will be your friends from Canada? Welcome to Penraven, both of you."

Glen felt uncomfortable, out of place. Perhaps if he had been an officer, preferably a commander or better, he would have felt more at home. But the butler's welcome seemed genuine enough.

"Thank you, sir," Glen said. "It's our pleasure."

Mr. Crane chuckled. "You don't say 'sir' to me; save that for Sir Godfrey. I'm just Mr. Crane. Come away in. I'm sure Martha has a pot of tea and some sandwiches ready to tide you over until dinner. You will be tired after your trip." It was a statement rather than a question, so Glen didn't respond. Actually neither of them was the least bit tired.

Mr. Crane led them through a hall into the kitchen where a round, flour-dusted woman welcomed them with a beaming smile.

"Glen, isn't it? Susan told me about you. And your friend all the way from Canada. I'm Martha and here's ... " she hesitated, looked around. "Now where's she gone? She was here a minute ago. Anyway she'll be here in a minute. Lucy, I mean. Now you two gents just sit yourselves down at the table. I have a nice cup of tea for you both and some scones and jam. Just help yourselves. Susan, why don't you join your friends? Jake can look after the chores for tonight. We're having roast beef and Yorkshire pudding for dinner

— our own beef. That's the advantage of living on a farm. And never you mind, Susan. I know you liked the beast but that's what beef cattle are for. You daren't get too fond of them. Ah, here's Lucy."

A young girl with blond hair and dark pools of eyes smiled and nodded.

"Wow!" whispered Ding to himself. Then aloud, "Nice to meet you, Lucy. I'm Ding and this is Glen."

She smiled shyly. "Nice to meet you . . . "

"Now," said Martha briskly, "it's time you had something to eat. Susan can show you to your rooms later. Lucy, see that they get whatever they need." She indicated the table. It was a plain wooden table with no napkins or placemats, with plain plates, cutlery and salt and pepper shakers. "This is where the help eats. Nothing fancy. You will be treated like gentlemen in the dining room for dinner, but I'm sure this will serve for a snack."

"When you are used to the lower deck grub," Glen assured her, "this is great. We often have to do with spam, or square eggs and red lead."

"Spam I know," said the cook. "But what in the world are square eggs and — what did you say? — red lead?"

"Square eggs are dehydrated eggs cut in squares and red lead is stewed tomatoes. Common fare for us when we're on convoy duty." Glen found himself sitting opposite Susan. Her hair, he realized, was not black, but a midnight brown and the sunlight streaming through the window behind her picked out auburn highlights. What is it, he wondered, that makes her so beautiful. Her features, taken one by one, seemed normal — except possibly those eyes. Lovely hair, yes, straight nose, small chin. Her lips were certainly not the cupid bow type preferred by advertisers, and one tooth was slightly crooked, but when she smiled, it was a heart-melting smile. And when all these features were added up, she was, well, beautiful. How come Ding seemed more interested in the girl Lucy? Not that Glen minded. After all, there was no accounting for tastes.

"Lucy," said Glen, "why don't you join us? We have everything we need so you don't have to wait on us."

Lucy hesitated, looking at Martha. The cook nodded. "You go ahead, Lucy."

She sat beside Susan, shyly.

"I didn't realize that you Canadians wear the same uniform as the Royal Navy," said Susan. "Why is that?"

"Because we're still regarded as colonials, I guess," said Glen. "It's embarrassing at times, when you realize that the uniform commemorates one of *your* heroes — Nelson."

"How does it do that?" asked Lucy.

"The three stripes on the collar commemorate Nelson's three great victories," explained Ding. "Like Trafalgar — "

"And Camperdown," added Glen.

"And the Nile, I suppose," murmured Susan.

"Yeah, I guess. And this black silk thing was added at the time of Nelson's funeral and we still wear it today."

"Don't you have any Canadian heroes?" asked Lucy.

"Sure we do. Maurice 'The Rocket' Richard."

"And Charlie Conacher," added Glen, a supporter of the Maple Leafs.

"And Howie Morenz."

"And Syl Apps."

"I never heard of any of those," said Susan. "Who were they?"

"Hockey players. Those are our Canadian heroes." Glen laughed. "Actually it's rather embarrassing sometimes. We even have the same flag as the RN: the white ensign. So we paint huge maple leaves on our funnels to let everyone know who we are."

"Some day," said Ding, "we'll have our own flag and uniforms, but right now there are more serious things to think about. Like the war."

"Surely with the invasion going well, it won't last too long now," said Susan hopefully.

"It's a long way to Berlin, and there's still the Pacific and the Japs," reminded Ding. "That's where we're going unless something unexpected happens."

"Oh. You're going to the Pacific, are you?" Susan bit her lip. "I'm sorry. We tend to forget that."

"Maybe something unexpected *will* happen," said Glen hopefully. "With new inventions almost every day — like the doodlebugs — you never know what they'll think of next."

Chapter Three

"THE DOODLEBUGS, as you call them, are nothing compared to what's coming." Sir Godfrey was seated in a deep armchair from which he surveyed the two sailors. They were seated self-consciously in their own comfortable chairs, one on each side of a huge fireplace. Above the fireplace was the portrait of a man who was obviously one of the present Sir Godfrey's ancestors. He had the same fiery red hair, military moustache and lowering brows. On the mantle shelf were the pictures of two more Trevours, one an army officer, the other with the air force. Again Glen felt out of place. He should have been an officer with gold braid to his elbow to be in a place like this. But Sir Godfrey didn't seem to mind the fact that they were mere able seamen. "You realize that it's the boffins who are going to win this war."

"The boffins, sir?"

"Yes. The scientists. The inventors. The ones who design the latest weapons, and who design defences against the enemy's latest weapon. The fastest fighter plane, the longest range bomber, the best tank — and how to combat them. You must have experienced this race in the navy."

"Oh yes. The Germans came up with the snorkel so the U-boats wouldn't have to stay on the surface for hours to recharge their batteries, and the acoustic torpedo so they wouldn't have to take several sightings before firing."

"Right. And our side came up with a defence against that, didn't we?"

"Oh sure. Nothing very complicated. A noise maker to tow behind the ship that makes more noise than the screws so the torpedo hits that and blows up. But of course if we're going fast that thing makes so much noise our asdic is use-less. So we keep a depth charge on a low setting to drop over the stern and set off the torpedo at a safe distance. That's what happened to our ship. Except that we already had weakened bottom plates and the explosion of the charge and the torpedo were a bit too much."

"And," added Ding, "it was one of our latest weapons that got us the U-boat. The squid. With the old depth charges you had to be going fast to avoid your own explosions and that way you lost contact with the U-boat. With the squid we can creep up on them slowly, keeping contact, then fire the charges ahead."

Sir Godfrey nodded. "That's what I mean. Invention and counter-invention. You experienced the doodlebugs. They're hard to deter. Anti-aircraft guns explode a few of them in mid-air, and some of the RAF pilots are having fun flying alongside them and tipping them over so they fall into the sea. My boy Cedric". — he vaguely indicated one of the photos on the mantel shelf — "told me about that. They're a nuisance but they're certainly not going to win the war at this late date. But there's a new flying bomb — the first one, I think, came down the other day, one of their liquid fuel rocket bombs."

Glen cleared his throat. "You're right, sir. I'm pretty sure it was one of those, maybe the first one, that came down on the village of Hook." He touched his still bandaged cheek and indicated Ding's forehead. "That's how we got these. It hit the tracks beside our train, and left a deep crater — deeper than anything a doodlebug would leave."

"Oh yes, that would be it." There was excitement in his voice. "There's no defence against them because they're un-detectable until they explode. They fly at a tremendous height at tremendous speed and their explosive power is un-believable. They're going to kill a lot of civilians, but again, they're coming too late to affect the outcome of the war. The Germans are putting up a stiff resistance, but our troops will sooner or later — sooner, I hope — capture the launching sites of the flying bombs."

Sir Godfrey pulled himself out of his chair, went to the window and looked out on the fields, standing with his hands clasped behind his back. "There are amazing inventions coming in the near future, lads," he said, without turning. "Those rockets are the forerunners of things to come — even someday putting a man on the moon. Sooner or later our blockbuster bombs will be replaced by a single bomb that will destroy a city. We can only hope that either the war ends before that is perfected, or our side comes up with it first. But there is another weapon that scares me even more than that."

Glen and Ding looked at each other. Glen whistled soundlessly. "What is that, sir?"

Sir Godfrey turned. His face was set. "Germ warfare. You know what that is? Living micro-organisms like anthrax bacillus or plague bacteria or poisonous toxins deliberately let loose on the enemy to infect them — civilians and armed forces alike. It is horrible to think of. You've heard of the bubonic plague of the Middle Ages? Millions died worldwide of what they called the Black Death. Well, that could be let loose today with the same result. Both sides have the capability. They are ideal weapons with tremendous psychological impact and far cheaper than airplanes and tanks and bombs. There are problems with it. The Japanese used it on Chinese civilians and soldiers, killing thousands. But it backfired. The wind changed and the germ-laden mist killed almost as many Japanese." He paused, shaking his head almost in despair. "As I said, both the Axis and the Allies have the capability. Who would use it first? Not us. But if in desperation, *they* use it, we might also, in retaliation. But that would be the destruction of everything we have accomplished over the years. The bubonic plague, or something even worse, spreading like wildfire, infecting millions on both sides in a short space of time. It is unthinkable."

"But surely," Glen gulped, "surely no one would be so insane as to let something like *that* loose anywhere."

"We sincerely hope you are right. If — no, let's say *when* — the Nazis are finally cornered like savage beasts, there is no telling what they will do."

It was at that moment that Mr. Crane entered the room. "Dinner is served, sir," he said formally.

"Thanks, Crane. Come, lads. Enough doom and gloom for one evening. Let's see what you can do with some good Cornish beef."

The boys soon showed him that they were capable of making good Cornish beef disappear in short order. At Sir Godfrey's invitation Susan had joined them at the table. Lucy hovered in the background, shaking her head at Ding's silent invitation to join them as well. Evidently her place was in the background, making sure everything was in order. There was little conversation until after the first course, and then after some apple dumpling had been disposed of, Sir Godfrey pushed back his plate.

"Have you any plans for your friends' visit, Miss Barclay?"

"Yes sir, we're going to the dance in the church hall this evening. Then we'll see. I'm not sure how long they will be able to stay. Do you know, Glen?"

"We have another week before we have to report back to the base," said Glen. "We're wondering, sir, if we might be permitted to explore this great house. We have very few mansions like this in Canada. Not with the history behind this one."

"Well, certainly. You're welcome. I'm afraid you will find much of it in poor condition. It was built with money from the tin trade, but that ran out so I must either find a lot of money to fix it up or, perhaps, convert it into flats. I'm not looking forward to that, but I may not have much choice. You're staying in the servants' quarters — right? And I'm living in this wing, with my family when the boys are home. The west wing is vacant and rundown, but you are welcome to look it over. You may find it interesting. Queen Victoria stayed here at one time. Her room is still furnished as it was for her visit, but otherwise it's left to the dust, and mice probably. The furnishings are covered with dust sheets. Just ask Crane. He'll give you the keys. Tell him I told him to."

"Thank you, sir. Is it true that the house is — or was — haunted?"

"Ah. You've heard that, have you? Well, if any place has a right to be haunted I suppose Penraven does."

Glen's interest quickened. "What do you mean, sir?"

"This house was built on the site of an ancient castle, Polgarth, a twelfth-century castle complete with a bottle dungeon. Do you know what that is?" Glen shook his head. "It's a dungeon shaped like a bottle with a narrow neck opening down into a wider hole. Prisoners were dropped into it through the narrow bottleneck and left to rot. The Polgarths backed the wrong side in the Civil Wars and the Roundheads came and razed the castle to the ground. Some of the Polgarths foolishly sought refuge in the bottle dungeon, and of course they were sealed inside, with predictable results.

Apparently the ghosts of both Sir Andrew and his dame were seen drifting around the estate a few times, vanishing through solid walls, that sort of thing. But neither one has been seen for many years. Now it seems my grandfather comes back occasionally and wanders the halls or disturbs visitors in their sleep. I remember a few odd happenings years ago, but not lately." He chuckled. "Make of it what you will, lads. People who *want* to see ghosts often will. Well, if you're going to the dance, you will be wanting to get away. Have a good time. Miss Barclay, take any time off you need. Jake and the boy can handle things."

"Yes, thanks. He already offered. Come along then, boys. We'll be on our way."

Chapter Four

THE STAIR LEADING to the servants' sleeping quarters was
nothing like the one the boys had glimpsed on their visit
with Sir Godfrey in the centre wing, which was wide, sweeping and carpeted. This one was narrow, steep and bare.

Susan led Glen and Ding up to the second floor and
showed them their rooms: two identical, plain rooms each
with a bed, a table and chair and a chest of drawers. The
walls were decorated with prints of Cornish scenery, rocky
coastlines, steep, cobbled village streets, wild moorlands.
There was a bathroom at each end of a long hallway from
which doors opened to more of the same identical rooms.

"Here you are," she said. "Plain but comfortable. We should leave in twenty minutes or so to go to the dance."

"Tell us about the dance," urged Ding. "You said it was for servicemen?"

"That's right. There are both army and air force bases within fifteen miles of here and the boys come to relax, dance, sing, write letters. It's dry, of course, no beer or liquor, because it's in a church hall, but it's well attended anyway — at least it was. Not so many come now, since many of the men who came are now on the continent with the invasion. Still, you should enjoy it. You may be the only representatives of the navy."

"Why is that?"

"Well, even though we're right on the coast, the nearest navy base is Plymouth and that's forty or fifty miles away."

"One thing," said Ding. "There's two of us and just one of you. D'you suppose Lucy could come along too?"

Susan's blue eyes twinkled. "If Martha will let her. She's Lucy's boss. There's a good chance she will. I'll ask, then go and harness Charlie to our chariot. Twenty minutes."

They heard the music as they approached the hall, the swinging big band sound.

"Ah," said Ding in appreciation from the back of the cart where he sat on a bed of hay beside Lucy. "That sounds like Glen Miller."

"That's right. And we have records by Tommy Dorsey and

Bennie Goodman and so on. And vocals by Sinatra and Crosby of course. And Vera Lynn and Gracie Fields. Oh we've got a great variety. Even so, we like to do our own singing. Listen."

They sat for a moment, outside the door to the hall, listening. The recording had stopped, and then there came the sound of many men singing the popular song. "I've got sixpence, jolly jolly sixpence ..."

The four of them joined in as Susan hitched Charlie to a post, and then led them into the hall.

As she had predicted there were a number of soldiers and airmen seated at tables around the hall with a few girls of each service. At some tables, civilian girls had joined the servicemen, and more women were at an open window where they served tea and coffee and buns. There appeared to be rivalry, more or less friendly, between the two groups of servicemen. One group singing "O happy is the day when the *airman* gets his pay" was almost, but not quite, drowned out by the other group roaring "happy is the day when the *soldier* gets his pay, as we go rolling, rolling home."

Glen and Ding were ready to join in with the word *sailor* in the appropriate place but the song ran out before they had a chance.

They were making their way to a table when a sergeant in khaki saw them.

"Hoi!" he shouted. "Here's Susan with the navy in tow. Let's hear a navy song for a change."

Glen and Ding looked at each other. "What could we sing? Our version of the sixpence song?"

"No," said Ding. "Something different."

"The only navy song I know is 'Wavy Navy.'"

"You mean 'Roll along Wavy Navy'?" Susan's eyes lit up. "I know that. Come on." She indicated a piano in the corner. "I'll play for you. We'll jazz it."

"You play the piano? And you can jazz 'Wavy Navy'?"

"Yes, I play the piano, and yes, I can jazz anything. Come along. Lucy, you come too. Come on, you two. Sing."

> *Roll along, Wavy Navy, roll along, roll along,*
> *Roll along, Wavy Navy, roll along.*
> *If you ask us who we are, we're the RCNVR,*
> *Roll along, Wavy Navy, roll along.*

In a moment everyone joined in to Susan's upbeat playing, singing the verse three times to whoops and clapping. A moment's pause then she began to play the popular tune "In the Mood."

Ding turned to Lucy. "May I have this dance, Miss Fenwick?"

She grinned. "You may, sir," and she was swept away onto the floor. They were joined at once by more couples.

Glen stood by the piano, humming the tune. Susan looked at him.

"You have a great voice," she said. "I'll bet you sing solos sometimes."

"Well, yes, I have done, on occasion," he admitted. "When I couldn't get out of it. That is, when my mum and dad insisted, to show me off to our relatives."

"What if I insisted now? Would you sing a solo here? For me?"

Glen gulped. He would do almost anything for her, he thought. *Almost.* But here in front of all these servicemen?

"Gee, I don't know. I don't know many popular songs and I'll bet that's what they would want — if anything. They would rather dance."

"Excuses!" she said. She was still playing "In the Mood." "You wait. After they've been dancing for a time there's nothing they'll like better than listening to 'I Walk Alone.'"

"O sure. With Lily Ann Carol singing it, who wouldn't? But I'm no Lily Ann Carol. They wouldn't want to listen to a guy singing that."

"No, maybe not," she conceded. "But we'll think of something."

Out on the floor several couples, including Ding and Lucy, were jitterbugging enthusiastically. Glen and Susan watched them, and as she brought the tune to a close, she and Glen applauded the dancers.

"How about a cup of tea — or whatever you prefer?" She waved acknowledgment of the applause she received for her playing, and led Glen to the refreshments while a Tommy Dorsey record was put on the player.

She accepted a cup of tea while Glen opted for cocoa. He

picked out a scone and a piece of pound cake for each. They were sitting down at a table when a voice called out to her.

"Miss Barclay. May I have a moment?"

"Reverend Farlow!" Glen noted the pleasure in her voice as a tall, slim, dark-haired man in a clerical collar limped across the floor towards them with a hesitant step.

"Don," the newcomer corrected, with a grin, as he held out his hand.

"If you call me Miss Barclay what do you expect? All right — Don. I would like you to meet two friends of mine, of my brother, actually, but now mine too. From Canada. This is Glen Cassley and that's Ding Dong cutting a rug out there on the floor. No kidding, that's what you must call him. He won't answer to anything else. Glen, this is the Reverend, or rather, Don Farlow, curate."

"Just to set the record straight I'm just a temporary assistant to the vicar." The man's grip was firm. "Pleased to meet you. It's a nice change to have the navy represented. I heard you singing before the whole gang drowned you out. You sounded good."

He pulled up a chair. "Tell me how your brother happens to have two Canadian sailors as friends, Susan."

She explained while the curate listened. He turned to Glen. "So you experienced the flying bombs in Croydon. That's something we haven't had to worry about here in Cornwall. Those bandages on your face — is that a souvenir of the doodlebugs?"

"Well, no, as a matter of fact. This was courtesy of the new rocket bomb."

"You mean you were there where it hit? Wow! They're calling them V2 bombs. I guess it was common knowledge that the Jerries were working on them and they would be hitting us sooner or later. Some of my pals were having fun flipping the doodles into the channel and telling me what fun I'm missing. They won't be able to do that to the V2s."

"Oh. You mean you were in the air force?"

"Yes. Until I was invalided out. They're calling it the Battle of Britain now. A wizard Jerry fighter pilot shot me down and gave me a bum leg to remember him by. But in spite of what they're saying it's mighty dicey work catching up to the buzz bombs. Only the latest Spitfire and the American Mustang are fast enough, then you have to fit your wing under the bomb's and flip it." He took a sip of tea and paused as if to change the subject. "You'll be having a relaxing time at Penraven, I hope?"

Glen grinned. "We *will* have, I expect. We just arrived this afternoon and haven't had time to relax. We're looking forward to our stay, including exploring the mansion."

"Exploring Penraven?" Don Farlow looked at him sharply. "Any particular reason why you want to explore an old house like that?"

"Well, it *is* old. We don't have many buildings that old in Canada, not with a history like Penraven has. And there's a hint that it may be haunted. *That's* interesting."

Don Farlow raised his eyebrows. He looked at Susan. "Have you been telling them ghost stories?"

"Me? No. I don't really know anything about it. Oh, I understand that it's supposed to be haunted, but I've never met up with anything eerie or spectral or unusual. It was something a man Glen met on the train said that started it, wasn't it, Glen?"

"That's right. This man, Jim Peters is his name, is writing a book about Cornwall manor houses and he mentioned that most of them have resident ghosts. Said he figured Penraven would have one — be haunted, I guess you might say. And sure enough, there is, or has been at least, stories of ghosts at Penraven."

"And this Jim Peters, is he going to investigate Penraven?"

"I expect so. He's staying at the Grey Gull just now — "

At that moment Ding and Lucy arrived at the table, flushed and breathless.

Introductions were made as Don and Glen stood until Lucy was seated and the two newcomers were served.

"We were talking about Penraven, the house, I mean," said the Reverend Farlow. "Some mention was made of the fact that it is supposed to be haunted — "

"Oh yes, it is," broke in Lucy. "There's even a haunted room. In the west wing. I know. My mum told me about it. She worked in Penraven for years and got me the job as maid before she left. She told me so many stories about the room that I decided to find out if there was anything to it. My friend Amy and I were going to spend a night there just to find out." She grimaced, shaking her head. "We stayed there for about two hours, then we ran. I don't know if it's really haunted, but there is something strange about that room."

"Like what?"

"Oh, I don't know. It's hard to explain. There were strange noises — bumps, scrapes, things like that, then the most awful shriek — not very loud, rather faint and fading out. Real scary. And the room got *cold*! As if icy fingers were reaching for you. Amy and I *ran*. We won't go in there again, I can tell you."

"Interesting," murmured Don Farlow. "When did this happen? Recently?"

"Oh, about two months ago. No one else knew; we didn't tell anyone. We weren't supposed to be in that part of the house."

"That'll teach you," grinned the curate. "This Jim Peters, Glen. What did he look like?"

"About your height. And build. But he's blond. Nice guy. Why?"

"Sounds like an interesting man. Maybe I'll meet him at Penraven." He turned to Susan. "Sir Godfrey's a member of St. Mark's parish, isn't he?"

"Definitely," nodded Susan. "There's a Trevour pew and he's in it most Sundays. Penraven money built most of it in the first place."

"Good. Then I should call on him. A pastoral visit. I'll see if I can work it into my schedule tomorrow."

He pushed his chair back. "What's the drill now, Susan? I was just told to be here and keep an eye on things. We close down at midnight. Correct?"

"That's right. We usually sing one from the hymn sheets and the vicar closes with a benediction. Some of the men will have left before that, of course, but there's always a few still here. They like a short prayer, especially since many of them know they'll be in the thick of the fighting very soon."

"Right. I'll ask the vicar to look after that. I have things to do. It's been nice meeting you, boys. No doubt I'll see you again."

The music had changed from jitterbug music to "Long ago and Far Away."

"Would you like to dance, Susan?"

She nodded. "Let's."

Glen forgot everything else then, except the closeness of Susan. She moved easily and gracefully, humming the tune, smiling at Glen. Then, when the music came to an end she led him back to their table.

"It's odd," she said, looking up from the rim of her tea cup. "All this time at Penraven and I never gave hauntings or ghosts a thought, and now suddenly it seems to be everyone's favourite topic. You and Ding, this Mr. Peters, Lucy, even Don Farlow. Speaking of the curate, I wonder why he's here. St. Mark's is a small parish and the vicar is very competent and popular as far as I know. And I know it quite well. I've played the organ once or twice when the regular organist was sick and I got along very well with Reverend

Stanwell, the vicar. And he never mentioned anything about an assistant. Then suddenly there is one, out of the blue."

"Well, I suppose there could easily be an explanation."

"Yes, there could," she admitted. "But there's something else. Did you notice Reverend Farlow, when he left here and went over to the door?"

"No, I wasn't watching him. Why?"

She leaned forward. *"He forgot to limp."*

"What? What do you mean?"

"What I say. You saw him come in. He limped, quite noticeably, didn't he?" Glen nodded. "But when he crossed the floor to go out there was no limp at all. No sign of one."

Glen shrugged. "Depends on the wound. Sometimes the pain comes and goes. I expect that's what happened."

"Yes, of course." She laughed. "Anyway that's a waltz they've put on the player. Shall we? One more dance?"

At a quarter to twelve, the lunch counter was closed. Some of the servicemen and women left, but a number remained.

"They want the hymn and benediction," said Susan. "Where's the vicar?"

"I don't know. But we could start the hymn, couldn't we? Where are the song sheets?"

She went to the piano and brought one back. "The Navy Hymn is on it. 'Eternal Father, Strong to Save.' You must know that one. You could lead. Couldn't you?"

"O sure. That's one hymn I know. We sing it at every church service and Divisions. First and last verses. And I'll make a minor change in the last line, just so the air men don't feel left out."

"What do you mean?

"Instead of 'Glad hymns of praise from land and sea' we'll make it 'Praise in the air, on land and sea.' You will announce it, will you? They seem to be expecting you to take over."

Susan sighed. "All right. I hope one of the clergy is here by the time we're finished. If not, who's going to lead in prayer?"

"We could ask for volunteers. You never know who might step forward."

She looked skeptical. "Let's hope we don't have to."

Glen was looking over the hymn on the song sheet. "Wait a minute. I think we have the answer. Let's just sing this hymn together, the two of us. I'd say it's both a prayer and benediction. And if anyone wants to join in, the words are here. After the Navy Hymn, of course. Just at the closing."

"Let me see. Oh yes, I know that one. It fits":

God be with you till we meet again.
When life's perils thick confound you,
Put unfailing arms around you.
God be with you till we meet again.

God be with you till we meet again.
Keep love's banner floating o'er you,
Smite death's threatening wave before you.
God be with you till we meet again.

"Yes," said Susan. "I think that would work very well. Thanks, Glen."

He grinned. "It's a pleasure. I never expected to be planning anything like this, but I like working with you. Even if it means singing in front of a bunch of pongoes and flyboys. Let's go."

Chapter Five

GLEN AWOKE EARLY to the sound of wind buffeting against the windows. He could see grey clouds scudding across a patchy sky, and a tree outside the window was bending before the power of the wind, reaching agitated branches to scratch at the window pane.

The window looked out on two barns and a smaller shed and, as he watched, Susan appeared from the shed, followed by eager chickens as she scattered feed over the ground. The wind clutched at her, tossing her hair, and she had to bend low to make sure the chicken feed hit the ground before it was snatched away by the wind. She paused for a moment, watching the feeding before she turned away to one of the barns.

Glen and Ding had brought a pair of dungarees each to save their uniforms and he donned his now and headed out his door, down the stairs. The kettle was on the stove, murmuring, just off the boil, the table was set for breakfast but there was no one about. He went outside.

The wind caught at him. He fought his way against it towards the barns. He had almost reached the first one when Susan emerged. She was carrying a pail this time. A milking pail, Glen guessed. It was a moment before she saw him.

"Glen!" she exclaimed, her eyes lighting up. "My! You're up early."

"Not really," he said. "This is my favourite time of day. The morning watch, four o'clock to eight. That way you see the sunrise, every one different, depending on where you are. How about you? Do you have to get up this early every day?"

"Oh yes. The chores, you know. Feeding the livestock, milking the cows. We have sixteen to milk right now, but the boys are looking after that so I have more time to spend with you and Ding. Just a moment."

She turned back, called out something to someone in the barn, set the pail down just inside the door and turned back to Glen.

"Listen!" She held up a warning hand. "What do you hear?"

"The wind," he said, at once. "And more than that. That booming sound. It must be the surf!"

"Right! On a windy day like this you can hear it plainly

even with the house between you and the sea. Come along."
She held out her hand. "I'll show you."

He had thought it must be an east wind, the way it had
swirled about him between the house and the barn, but as
they rounded the mansion and headed west it struck them
with full force. Heads bent low keeping near the wall for its
meagre protection, they climbed a gentle slope towards where
the world seemed to stop, and beyond it nothing but sky.

Glen stopped once, listening, perplexed. "That noise — it
must be more than the surf."

She nodded. "I'll explain when we get closer."

They left the house behind and battled their way upwards
until she stopped. "We're near the cliff edge here," she warned,
"so be careful. There's no fence. Sometimes the rocks are
slippery. They'll be wet with spray today. Come this way."

She led him diagonally to where there was a dip then a
gap in the rock face, where they could crouch down out of
the worst of the wind. In a moment their faces were wet with
spray. Before them the cliff face dropped perpendicularly to
the shore and beyond was the raging Atlantic Ocean.

"That noise . . . " said Glen. It was a deep, hollow, booming reverberation. "What *is* it?"

"Remember what I told you about the cliff being riddled
with caves? Well we're right on top of a cave, a big one. The
waves are pounding into it. That's what you hear. There are
a lot of caves opening off the big one, like a honeycomb apparently, reaching away back no one knows how far. If there
ever was a usable path down the cliff there's no sign of it

now; Sir Godfrey says the smugglers that used the caves must have rigged up some sort of derrick to hoist the goods up from the shore. Smuggling was big business, almost respectable." She turned and looked out to sea where the breakers tossed their white caps into the air, to have them snatched away by the wind. A few seagulls, calling their harsh cries, struggled momentarily against the wind, then rode it on outstretched wings wherever it might take them.

"It's wild today," she said. "Do you like it like this?"

He nodded. "Oh yes. I love the ocean in all its moods. Listen":

> To stand once more on a wind-swept shore
> and hark to the surf's resurgent roar
> with raucous seagulls crying,
> where the walloping winds their revels keep
> and seas roll in from the booming deep
> with jewelled mains aflying.

"Oh." She thought for a moment. "I don't think I've heard that one before."

"I know you haven't. It's never been published."

She looked at him, eyes wide. "*You* wrote it, didn't you!"

He nodded. "Don't tell my shipmates. Not even Ding. It's a secret vice. The sea brings it out in me — that and my dinner on a day like this."

She laughed. "All right. I won't tell anyone as long as you

promise to give me a copy of the whole thing. That was just one verse, wasn't it? Yet you lived many miles from the ocean. I know. We looked up your home town on a map. It must be hundreds of miles."

"About a thousand, actually. But I read lots of sea stories that intrigued me. And you would be surprised at the number of boys from the prairies who joined the navy. They lived even farther from the ocean than I did. Much farther. The sea's fascinating and terrifying at the same time." He looked out on the great white-topped breakers rolling in to throw themselves at the shore, flinging spray high in the air, to fall like rain on the clifftop. "I don't think I will ever get used to it."

He turned to look back at the bulk of Penraven House. "About the caves," he said. "Do you think they might go back as far as the mansion?"

"I suppose it's possible," she said. She looked at him curiously. "Why?"

He shrugged. "Just a thought."

The house stood about fifty metres from the clifftop, the blank windows of the west wing staring at them.

"If he, Sir Godfrey, ever does turn that part of the house into apartments — or flats, as you call them — he should get a good rent for them. Must be a grand view, especially from the second or third floors. That is if you like a view of the ocean. He said we could explore the house if we wanted to. Would you join us?"

"Of course. And we might ask Lucy where the 'haunted room' is. You want to check that out, don't you?"

He grinned. "Yes. Another thing. There's one of those ruins you called 'Cornwall castles' over there beyond the barns." He pointed to where it loomed against the sky. "I'd like to take a closer look at that. Okay?"

"Sure, if you like. You won't see much. They can be very dangerous so this one at least is kept securely locked. In some places shafts and workings are unmarked and unfenced and shafts drop hundreds of feet and then run for miles."

With the wind behind them helping them along, they soon passed the barns, crossed a pasture field and climbed a slope to where the grey granite building, like a tall castle keep, stood beside a towering chimney.

"This was the engine room where they controlled the lift and access to the shafts." Steps led up to a massive door that was, as she had said, securely locked, but there were open window gaps above it. "Shafts run for miles, quite possibly all the way to the shore and out under the sea. In the other direction, they might go far enough to meet up with shafts from that other stack you can see on that far hill."

"Wow," said Glen in awe. "An underground honeycomb. And caves. Is there never a cave-in?"

She shook her head. "All this granite is as firm as . . . well, as firm as a rock. Mining was a terrible life. They worked for a long time just with ladders leading down into the depths before they introduced steam lifts. And with the dust, dirt and darkness, disease was rife. Few lived beyond forty, even if they survived accidents. It was a good thing when surface tin was found in Europe and these mines were forced to close, although it put thousands out of work."

They turned away from the ruins and headed back into the wind.

"Breakfast must be ready by now," said Susan. "Let's see if Ding is up."

Glen didn't answer for a moment. He was thinking of caves and mine shafts, and another hole in the ground: a bottle dungeon.

Chapter Six

THE NAZI SUBMARINE U-555 lay on the ocean floor, waiting.
To her crew it was a welcome respite from the nerve-wracking hunt for prey, the search for convoys and the demoralizing sound of depth charges exploding nearby, creeping closer. The branch of the navy in which they proudly served had almost won the war single-handedly in the earlier years, sending ship after ship to the bottom and threatening to starve the United Kingdom into submission. But gradually with the inexhaustible ability of the Allies to build more ships, merchant and escort alike, the tide had turned until the U-boats were on the defensive, battling in what most of them feared was a lost cause.

Still, there was one hope. Hitler had promised secret weapons that would save the Third Reich from defeat. The crew had heard about new unmanned bombs that were causing devastation to the enemy. But there had to be something more than that before it was too late.

To the captain of the U-boat in his lonely bunk, the wait on the ocean floor was exasperating. Normally he welcomed weather like this. Great rolling breakers tended to scatter a convoy over hundreds of miles of sea, sending the escort vessels off in all directions to round them up, leaving the individual ships easy prey for the lurking submarines. He fondly remembered one such occasion when a tanker, loaded with airplane fuel, had come into his sights. No need to wait, to take different sights to estimate her speed and direction. Simply release one of the new acoustic torpedoes. He had fired two, just to be sure. The result, one gigantic thunderclap of sound, and the tanker had disintegrated into a million pieces of steel and human flesh and blood. And, because of that, some Allied bombers would be left idle on a tarmac for want of fuel, saving war targets and innocent German women and children from death and destruction.

This time it was because of those same rolling breakers that he was forced to sit idle and wait for calmer weather, for there was a container taking up precious space in the torpedo room, containing he knew not what. He was not *supposed* to know. He knew only that he was to deposit it in a certain cave on the Cornish coast, when he received the signal, then get out of there fast. What happened then was up to someone on shore. Meanwhile he had to wait, and he hated waiting. There were too many ships out there to be sunk . . .

Chapter Seven

"EXPLORING PENRAVEN House will have to wait," said Susan at the breakfast table. "I must go to town to get some supplies for Cook. Would you like to come?"

"Sure." The boys were eager. "I'll drive," offered Ding. "Lucy can sit up front with me while you two sit in the hay in the rumble seat. Okay?"

"All right, if Cook can get along without Lucy." She looked enquiringly at Martha, who nodded.

"There's nothing that can't wait until you return. Away you go and have fun."

"Thanks. You three wait here, while I go and hitch Charlie to our chariot."

Glen, Ding and Lucy were still seated at the table a few minutes later when Susan called from outside.

"Let's go. Charlie and I can't wait all day." She looked enquiringly at Ding as the three emerged. "Do you still want to drive? Have you ever driven a horse before?"

"Sure. I mean, no, I haven't, but how difficult can it be?"

"You're right. There's nothing to it. Here. Get up and I'll show you."

Ding climbed nimbly into the front seat, helped Lucy up beside him, took hold of the reins and looked around. "Where's the whip?"

Susan laughed. "You don't need a whip for Charlie. Charlie would be insulted and refuse to move. Here. You pull on this rein if you want to go to the left — "

"Port," corrected Ding.

"I beg your pardon?"

"Not left. *Port!* This is a naval operation. We will operate with true naval efficiency."

"Oh," said Susan, sounding impressed. "And tug on this rein to go — what is it? *Starboard!* Is that right?"

"Good for you. We'll make a sailor of you yet, won't we, Glen? Now what do you say when you want to stop?"

"That," said Susan, "is the least of your problems. Charlie is always waiting for that command and anything will do. You could yell 'charge' or whisper 'whoa' and it's all the same to Charlie. If we're moving, any command means stop."

"Good. Now, you two get up into the hay and we're off to the races."

Glen sat beside Susan in the hay, not as close as he, at least, would have liked, but they were shoulder to shoulder. "All set," he called. "Cast off bow and stern lines. Anchors aweigh."

"Right. Okay, Charlie! You heard the man. Let's go."

Charlie didn't move.

"Come on," urged Ding. "*Giddyap*. Move! *En avant* in case you're French. What's the matter with the beast?"

"Perhaps we haven't got steam up yet," suggested Glen. "Get the chief stoker on the horn. They must be slacking off in the engine room."

Ding ignored him. "Susan," he yelped. "How do I get him moving?"

"You don't get *him* moving at all. She's a girl. Her full name is Charlene."

"Oh. I hadn't noticed. So what do I do? Compliment him — her — on her hairdo? Whisper sweet nothings in her ears? *Beg* her to please at least start in the right direction?"

For answer Susan put two fingers to her lips and let out a piercing whistle. Glen gripped the side of the cart, half expecting the horse to take off like a rocket. She didn't. But at least she moved. They were underway.

"That's it," said Susan. "You just have to whistle the right note, and Bob's your uncle."

"Eh? What? I don't have any uncle called Bob. What are you talking about?"

"It's an expression," she said. "'Bob's your uncle' means everything's under control. Don't ask me to explain it."

"You people are weird. What's our first port of call?"

"The grocery shop. You can't miss it."

"You'd be surprised at what I can miss," muttered Ding. "Lucy, you're the navigator. Are we headed in the right direction?"

"Since there's only one direction we *can* go, unless you turn right around, I would say we must be," reasoned Lucy, getting into the spirit of things. "Dead ahead. Is that how you say it? And sooner or later we will sight our target on the starboard side."

"Not target," corrected Ding. "Port of call. How are things back there on the quarterdeck?"

"'Shipshape and Bristol fashion,'" said Susan. "That's another of our 'weird' sayings I can't explain." She moved closer to Glen, their backs to the side racks. She grinned at him. "Somehow I don't think this is very ship-like in today's navy."

Glen sighed. "I'm afraid not, so I'll take advantage of it while I can," and he put his arm around her . . .

"Port in sight," reported Ding, too soon for Glen. "We'll pull alongside and heave to at the grocer's shop. Hands to stations for entering harbour. Liberty men fall in." And a few minutes later: "All ashore that's going ashore."

"That's us," said Susan, extricating herself. "Do I pass inspection?"

"With flying colours." Glen pulled himself up, jumped

down to the sidewalk and turned to help Susan, but she didn't need any help.

"Do the rest of you want to come in while I get things on the cook's list or do you want to explore on your own?"

"Lucy and I are going exploring," decided Ding. "There's a tea room down there and there may be some fancy cakes to sample."

"Some hope, in wartime, and you've just had your breakfast. Oh well . . . Are you coming with me, Glen? Okay, we'll see you two later."

They were turning into the shop when Susan stopped, looking down the street.

"There's Reverend Stanwell, the vicar. I think I'll talk to him. Come and meet him."

"Miss Barclay! How nice to see you!" The vicar's gentle face lit up. "And you must be the Canadian friend. I'm so pleased to meet you." His handshake was warm and firm, his face, beneath a shock of unruly white hair, beamed. "Are you enjoying your visit?"

"Very much, thank you. We were dancing in your parish hall last night. That was fun."

"Oh, that's good to hear. I couldn't be there myself. I hope my associate welcomed you."

"Yes, he did," said Susan, "but in the end he rather left us in the lurch. He went out before the last hymn and left us high and dry. Some of the chaps were still there waiting. Neither of us is used to praying in public. But we managed."

"I'm sorry to hear that. He shouldn't have left you like that. But he will only be here a short time."

"Where did he come from?" asked Susan. "I mean . . . do you really need an associate, sir?"

He chuckled. "No, you're quite right. I don't. He is here on a special mission. The bishop is thinking about having an orphanage in this area after the war. The war has left us with many orphans, as you know. Farlow is looking around to see if there are any existing buildings that might do. He has mentioned Penraven as a possibility, if Sir Godfrey is interested in selling. He seems like a nice young man. Was in the RAF but was shot down and crippled somewhat, as I expect you saw, and demobilized. I have no idea why he, or the bishop, chose this parish."

"Probably because everyone likes you and the church is run very well and is well attended," said Susan, sincerely. "I doubt if the same can be said about a lot of them."

The vicar actually blushed. "Well, thank you. That's very nice of you to say so, though I'm afraid it is not all that it seems on the surface. Parishes never are, being made up of human beings. And while we are in the complimentary mood I must thank you for all you do, playing the organ when Phoebe is unwell, and helping out on the piano at the dances." He turned to Glen. "We are very fortunate to have Susan helping out at Penraven and here at St. Mark's. How do you happen to know her?"

Glen explained his association with the family. "As it

turned out I haven't met Jack at all, but luckily Susan's in a job that isn't all that secret and Ding and I were able to come to Cornwall. It's been a great experience."

"I'm sure it has, for both you and Susan. Well, I must be on my way. I was going to call on Penraven this week but young Farlow has offered to go in my place. A chance for him to look over the building, as a possible orphanage. You may see him when he does. Maybe today."

They watched him go for a moment, then looked at each other again.

"So that explains Don Farlow's interest in Penraven. I wonder why he didn't tell us. I suppose it just never came up."

"If he comes to Penraven we'll have to watch him and see if he forgets to limp again," grinned Glen. "Now, what's on your list?"

Chapter Eight

"BEFORE YOU SET out on your exploration, let me tell you a little more about Penraven House," said Sir Godfrey. Lucy had once again been permitted to join Susan, Glen and Ding. "Today, we — that is, my boys and I, and the staff, of course — live in the east and central wings. Beyond the room in which I met you yesterday there is a ballroom, where, in times of peace, we sometimes entertain. There is a piano in there. Susan, you are welcome to play it any time you are free from your duties. In fact, I wish you would. I miss it since the boys left. They are both musical. Beyond it is the games room with billiard and tennis tables. There again you are welcome to entertain yourselves. Our living quarters are beyond that again and upstairs. Just what we will do in the future will have to be decided when the boys come home, if and when they marry.

"The west wing is the part that might interest you. It seems to have interested a man by the name of Peters who is somewhere in the wing just now. He's writing a book about Cornwall ghosts, came in yesterday to ask permission, and came back this morning to go through the west wing.

"As I told you there is a tradition that we are haunted, but as far as I am concerned it is nothing more than that. Tradition. There is one room known as the haunted room because of strange noises, but I have never heard anything that can't be explained. We just make sure we don't put any guests in there."

"We met Mr. Peters on the train," said Glen. "He mentioned the possibility of ghosts being here and that he would like to explore the house. Can you tell us a little more about the history? Penraven was built on the site of a ruined castle, you said. Were any of the ruins incorporated in the new building?"

Sir Godfrey shook his head. "Very little, if any, as far as I know. That, of course, was somewhat before my time. More than two hundred years. Were you thinking that there may have been some ghosts associated with Polgarth Castle that might still be hanging around?" He smiled. "Mr. Peters has some such idea. I don't know. I'm not familiar with the behaviour of ghosts."

"You mentioned before that the Polgarths hid in the bottle dungeon when the castle was captured and were shut in there and left there. Was it filled in when this house was built?"

Sir Godfrey shook his head. "No, I don't believe so. Just sealed, covered over and left, as far as I know. I'm not even sure where it is. I've never given it much thought."

"Thank you, sir." Glen turned to Susan. "Let's go and have a look around the west wing, then come back and you can play the piano for us."

She nodded. "If that's all right with Sir Godfrey?"

"My pleasure."

The west wing had been set aside for guests in the days of high entertaining. Bedrooms, some small, some elaborate, took up both the second and third floors. There was little furniture left in any of them and what there was, was covered in dust sheets. There were signs of mould where the rain had come in, and spider webs hung here and there undisturbed. One room, on the second floor, was identified as the room in which Queen Victoria had stayed. There was little to distinguish it from any of the others, except that it was still furnished. The bed was a canopy type and there was a rich tapestry on the wall, depicting a hunting scene, with one of the "Cornwall castles" dominating the horizon. The rest of the furniture was covered.

"It must have been quite a sight when the court met here

to party," said Ding, rather impatiently. "Now, Lucy, where's this haunted room you told us about?"

"Downstairs on the ground floor. The last room at the back, on the left." She looked at the others. "There's likely nothing about it in the daylight, but in the dark it is scary."

"Let's go see."

A broad stair with worn carpeting led them down to the main floor. Here the rooms were apparently more for meetings, with cloakrooms and bathrooms off each one and empty shelves lining the walls. As in the upstairs rooms, the few remaining pieces of furniture — desks and tables and chairs — were covered over. Each room was separated from the next by a walk-in cupboard.

They took only casual glances into each one until they reached the end of the corridor. Only one room remained.

"This is it," said Lucy. "The haunted room. We didn't like the idea of sleeping in a strange bed so we brought air mattresses and sleeping bags. We were determined to stay the night. We thought we wouldn't be scared of any ghosts. But when we heard the noises, it was too much. We ran."

Ding gallantly took her hand. "Never mind, Lucy. We'll see what's going on. There's four of us, and besides it's broad daylight. Let's go in."

Glen pushed the door open and they entered. It was a room not unlike the others. Dust covers hid a bed and two other articles of furniture, evidently chairs. There was a worn carpet on the floor. There was only one window, on the west side facing the ocean. Glen went to it and looked out. Beyond the ground sloping up to the clifftop, he could see the angry sea rolling in, flinging spray high in the air. He was standing there when they first heard it. First, it was a low moan, then a sudden, sharp shriek. And then nothing. They looked at each other. Lucy squeezed Ding's hand.

"Where did it come from?" It was hard to tell. They waited. It came again, not as loud this time. Eerie. Spooky.

"Okay," said Glen. For some reason he was whispering. "Let's suppose we had never heard that this room was haunted, that we didn't believe in ghosts anyway. Then we heard that noise. What would we think it was?"

A moment's hesitation, then Susan said, "The wind. Catching in something loose. Making it vibrate."

"Of course," said Ding. "That must be it. Was it windy the night you were here, Lucy?"

She shook her head. "I don't remember. Not like today anyway."

"It's always windy here, more or less." Susan was beside Glen, looking out. "If there's something loose it might not take more than a breeze to make *some* noise. Do you see something that might do it?"

"No. But it could be anything. Maybe around the corner on the back wall. It's impossible to tell where it's coming from. Was there anything else, Lucy? Do you remember?"

"A thud, like something falling, I think. But I suppose that could have been anything. Maybe in the room next door.

There are mice, maybe rats." She blushed. "I'm afraid Amy and I were scared of nothing."

"Hey!" objected Ding. "Don't say that. I wouldn't have had the nerve to try it in the first place. Well, Glen, do you think we've solved the mystery of the haunted room or is there more to it?"

Glen was looking around. "I was just thinking . . . It looks as if there has been someone else in here recently. There are footprints in the dust over there." He pointed. "Those aren't ours, and the rug has been lifted in that corner."

"You are quite right. The footprints are mine."

They spun round. Jim Peters was standing in the door-way.

"Oh. Hi! Mr. Peters . . . "

Chapter Nine

"RIGHT." JIM PETERS came into the room. He was grinning. "Thanks to you guys I've got some great ideas for my book. Penraven's the goods, believe me. It's a great story. I don't know how much Sir Godfrey has told you, so here goes. There was originally a castle on this site, Polgarth Castle. The village takes its name from that. The owner was the Earl of Crummin. His name was Polgarth but the earldom was that of Crummin. Don't ask me to explain those things. Anyway, the Polgarths backed the king in the civil wars and when the Roundheads won they came and sacked the castle. The story goes that the earl and his countess hid in the bottle dungeon. You know what that is? Okay. Now that, to my way of thinking, was a stupid thing to do. In the first place, the conquerors were sure to open the dungeon to release any of their men who might have been captured and incarcerated there, and they would have found the earl. And even if, for some reason, they didn't, can you think of any death worse than dying of starvation, or going mad, in a tiny black hole with absolutely no light whatever? I can't. I'd rather die on the scaffold any day.

"Then I heard that the ghosts of the earl and countess were seen. More than once. Now on the question of there really being such things as ghosts I have an open mind, but *this* set me to thinking." He was looking around the room as he spoke, his eyes finally resting on the floor. "Suppose those were not ghosts but real people. They had survived. But how could they? Could there possibly be a way out of a bottle dungeon? That doesn't make sense. Dungeons are hacked out of solid rock. But how about this one?" He indicated the window. "You know what's out there? Under that solid surface? A cave. A huge cave. It opens out on the ocean, of course. But how far back does it reach? Could it possibly reach all the way back to Polgarth Castle? Of course it could. Could the bottle dungeon have really had a connection to the cave? It wouldn't have been any use as a prison, of course, but maybe it wasn't meant to be that anyway. Just an escape hatch in case of invasion. Why not? I can see it now. The Roundheads swarming into the castle. The earl and countess making sure they are seen, then dropping down into the dungeon. The invaders triumphantly sealing the dungeon off forever. Never guessing, of course, that there was a way out."

He was grinning. "Now, something else I've been wondering about. Smuggling. Sir Godfrey doesn't know, or claims he doesn't, how the smuggled goods were brought up from the cave. He suggests a hoist. That is possible, of course. But why not through the bottle dungeon? As far as he knows, it was covered over when this house was built. But was it? Of course all this begs one question. Where is the entrance to it now?"

The four had been listening, fascinated. Glen spoke after a minute. "The haunted room would seem to be the answer to that. 'Haunted' purposely to keep people away maybe. To hide the smuggling operation. But I don't see any sign of an entrance. It would have to be the floor, wouldn't it? It looks as if the carpet was moved recently. Was that you?"

"Yes. You're right, of course. It would have to be the through the floor. I've taken the whole carpet up and the floor's solid enough, believe me. I was hoping you with your fresh look at the whole thing might have some other ideas."

They were all looking around with new purpose. "You checked the cupboard too, of course?"

"Oh yes. The floor's solid in there too." He opened the door to it. It was only a metre or so deep, the far wall separating it from the next-door cupboard.

Glen looked in. There were several hooks to accommodate clothes. He had a sudden idea. He reached in, took hold of one of them and pulled. Nothing. He tried all of them, but with no better result.

"Good idea," nodded Peters. "But no joy. However there's something else here." Up near the roof there was a light switch, but there didn't seem to be any light it might operate. He reached up and flicked it.

A panel in the wall slowly opened.

"Hey! Look at this." It opened into the adjoining room's cupboard.

"Interesting," commented Peters, failing to hide his excitement. "Trying to conceal the entrance. People like me will naturally think the entrance would be in the haunted room so we look there and give up. And in smuggling times, the police would have thought the same thing and given up. And all the time it's in the room next door. Smart! At least that's my guess. Let's look at the floor in *this* room."

They examined the floor in the cupboard first, but it was obviously solid. They went into the next room, moved the furniture back, and began to pull up the carpet. They were less than half done when Ding let out a whoop.

"Hey! Look here. The floor boards. They're different here. There's a square of boards running the opposite way. And look! An iron ring embedded in the floor. Give me a hand here, Glen."

The two of them grasped the iron ring and heaved. "It's coming," breathed Lucy, excited.

Peters was on his haunches watching. "It's not hinged.

Just resting on the underfloor. By George, you've got it. Let me help you . . . Here we go."

A four-foot square opened up, disclosing a black hole.

"It's the bottle dungeon," grinned Glen. "It must be."

"But there's no light," said Susan, disappointed. "There would be if it opened into the cave, wouldn't there?"

"No. There could be a curtain or something to hide the opening. Otherwise the earl and countess wouldn't have fooled the soldiers. We need a light."

"Right here." Peters produced a flashlight and turned it to shine down the black shaft. "It's a bottle dungeon all right. See how the neck opens out just like a bottle. And look. There's a ladder of sorts leading down into it. *That's* a modern addition, probably installed by the smugglers. Well, who's game to go down?"

"You better go first," said Glen. "It's your find. We'll follow if you want."

"Okay. Here goes." Peters lowered himself over the brink, feet reaching for the steps of the ladder. Then he climbed down until his feet reached the floor. He stopped, casting the light around. They heard a satisfied shout. "Got it!" His flashlight was extinguished, but now there was light flooding the dungeon.

"Come on down. You must see this."

A narrow opening led them into the cave itself. Here it was low and narrow, but it soon opened out, the roof reaching high above them. They could see all the way to where the

angry sea hurled itself into the entrance with a roaring sound
that echoed eerily throughout the cave. White-capped waves
rolled in, curling over, reaching, then reluctantly receding, to
gather themselves again for another try.

"The tide's in just now," said Peters. "It won't reach in so
far when it's out. I wonder how long this weather's going to
last. Anyone seen a weather report?"

"It's already slackening off," said Susan. "My guess is it
won't last more than another day. What do you think, Mr.
Peters? We haven't found any ghosts, but we may have found
the explanation for two ancient ghosts, the earl and countess. Will this go into your book?"

"Oh yes. Certainly. Thanks to all of you. You've been a big
help. I must get back to my digs and start typing it all up."

Chapter Ten

THE REVEREND DON FARLOW parked his Austin in the driveway and walked to the front door of Penraven. His limp slowed him down noticeably.

He hesitated for a moment, his hand on the bell pull, then he withdrew it and stepped back. He surveyed the front of the house, then turned and hobbled along beside a flower garden until he turned the corner and was looking at the outhouses. He withdrew a camera from his pocket and took several shots that would include the barns and fields beyond. A man came out of the barn, watched him for a moment, then approached.

"Hello. Oh. Reverend," he added, noticing the clerical

collar. He held out his hand. "I'm Jake Higgins. Can I help you?"

"Pleased to meet you, Jake. I'm Don Farlow, helping out at St. Mark's." He indicated his camera. "In case you're wondering about this I should tell you. There is a possibility that someday this property may be turned over to the church and transformed into an orphanage. Not for some time, of course. There's a war to win now. But the authorities would like some pictures to get an idea as to the extent and condition of the building and lands, before doing any serious negotiations. You work the farm, I suppose? Would you say it is good farmland?"

Jake was cautious. "Yes," he ventured, after a moment. "I would say it is good for growing produce, which would be good for feeding children. There's good pasture land and a good crop of hay this year. Which means good dairying. If it works out and you might need some help — "

"You don't need to worry on that score, Jake. Your job is safe, I'm sure. How far does the property extend?"

"You see yon mine adit? That is just over the line. There's fifty acres all together, as much as possible under cultivation since the war."

"Fine. Thank you very much, Jake. I will take a stroll over to the clifftop." He hesitated. "I understand there's a cave below the cliff. Can it be reached from the top?"

"Not less'n you're a fly, it can't. Not any more."

"Oh. Well, I'm no fly. Thanks again."

Don Farlow turned and limped along beside the wall of the house, climbing the incline, until he stood atop the cliff. The wind still whipped about him, and the waves were rolling in to fling spray skyward, but it was gradually slackening off. By tomorrow, he thought, it should be calm enough for a boat to reach the cave. He would have to check out the availability of boats for rent. He surveyed the terrain carefully, just in case Jake's estimate was incorrect, but he soon gave up any hope of climbing down the cliff.

He turned towards the house.

A few minutes later Don Farlow was ushered into the presence of Sir Godfrey. The latter was seated at a desk in a small room which appeared to be an office. He regarded his visitor with interest, as he rose to meet him with outstretched hand, then motioned him to a chair on the other side of the desk.

"I don't believe we are acquainted, sir," he said. "I am a great friend of the vicar, the Reverend Stanwell, of course. A fine man. I was not aware that another clergyman was in any way associated with St. Mark's." The tone of his voice suggested this was an unwelcome oversight on the part of the parish.

"No, no, I assure you," said the curate hastily. "I am strictly temporary, with a particular task. This is not a pastoral call. Reverend Stanwell will be calling on you again in the near future, I have no doubt. As you may be aware, the church is concerned for the welfare of the orphans caused by the war and the need for shelters and homes for them in the near future. One, we hope, will be established in Cornwall, and my task is to find suitable locations or, better still, existing buildings that might be bought and renovated. That, sir, is why I am here today. There is a rumour going the rounds that you might be interested in selling Penraven."

"Is there, indeed!" Sir Godfrey didn't seem all that surprised. "The operative word is 'might,' and a very slim 'might,' I must say. No, I haven't really considered *selling*, but now that you mention it, perhaps we should think about it. I have thought of renovating the west wing and converting it into flats. A very expensive proposition and not very inviting. But selling?" He shook his head. "Penraven has been in the family for generations. It is our home, and not lightly to be turned over to someone else, not even orphans, worthy as the cause may be. And of course no decision can be made one way or another until my boys come home. It is their home too, and one of them is soon to be married."

"I understand," nodded the curate. "But sir, as long as there is the possibility, I wonder if I might be given the permission to look over the house and grounds and report back to my superiors. If *they* aren't interested then there's the end of it."

"Certainly. A very good suggestion. It seems odd that there should suddenly be so many people interested in exploring our old home."

Don Farlow's eyes narrowed. "What do you mean, sir?"

"A writer left here not an hour ago. Writing a book about Cornwall ghosts. He heard that Penraven is haunted, and his explorations uncovered a most astonishing secret. One I never dreamed of and I have lived here all my life. There is a bottle dungeon below the house. *That* is no surprise. I knew there had been one under the original castle but assumed it was covered over when Penraven was built. The surprising discovery is that it was *not* a genuine bottle dungeon. It is a fake!"

"A fake? I don't understand. What is a fake dungeon?"

"I don't know if you are aware, but there is a huge cave below our cliff, a cave that actually reaches as far as this house. And the bottle dungeon is actually *open to the cave*! It was used, I assume, as an open shaft to bring up the smuggled goods in my grandfather's time, and before that it was *an escape hatch*! The original owners of Polgarth Castle used it to escape Cromwell's forces in the civil wars."

"Wait a minute!" Farlow could hardly contain his excitement. "You mean you can actually get into the cave from inside this house?"

"That is what I'm saying, yes. And to think it was there all this time and I was none the wiser. None of us knew, not even my boys, and they have explored the haunted room to discover the source of the 'haunting.'"

"The haunted room? Is that where the entrance to the dungeon is?"

"No. If it had been, my boys would most likely have discovered it. The entrance is actually in the room next door."

"Oh. I wonder . . ."

"I don't know what difference its existence would make to an orphanage. Is that what you're wondering?"

"Well, yes," nodded Reverend Farlow. "Perhaps if I could take a look at it?"

"Why not, if you wish. It will be common knowledge when Peters' book is published."

"Peters? Is that the writer you mentioned?"

"Yes. You know him?"

"Not really. How did he discover it, do you know?"

"He had the help of two young sailors who are staying here for a few days. Canadians, friends of our Land Army girl. They're either in the music room or the games room right now . . . " He hesitated a moment, listening. "At least one of them is in the music room. I can hear the piano. If you like, you could ask them to show you what they discovered."

Farlow hesitated a moment, then nodded. "Yes, if they would be willing, that would be fine."

"Very well. Just through that door and down the hall. Follow the sound of the piano."

Susan was playing "Till the Lights of London Shine Again" with Glen on the piano bench beside her singing what words he knew, "I'll keep your picture near me, a tender souvenir" and "dum de dum de dum dum" and "may God bless you, dear." Then humming before ending up with a triumphant "Till the lights of London shine again."

Don Farlow waited in the doorway until they came to the end. Then, clearing his throat he entered, clapping.

"Very good. Next time you come to the dance we'll have a solo, Glen. May I come in?"

"Of course," said Susan. "Just don't leave us in the lurch again. How is the leg? Still bothering you?"

"Oh yes. I'm afraid it's permanent." He limped over to stand beside them. "Have you heard I'm interested in Penraven as a possible future orphanage? I've been talking to Sir Godfrey and he was telling me about your discovery of the fake bottle dungeon. That was some find!"

"Yes. Very exciting. What does Sir Godfrey think of your idea for an orphanage?"

"He's undecided, of course. It's a big decision to make. But I have permission to explore the house for my superiors to decide if they're really interested. And he suggested you might be willing to show me the dungeon you found."

"Sure," offered Glen. "Be glad to. I wonder if Ding and Lucy would like to come too. Just a moment." They could hear the tap tap of the table tennis ball hitting the table in the room next door. It ceased for a moment when Glen entered with the invitation. Ding waved him away.

"You go ahead. Lucy vows she can beat me. I have to teach her a lesson. You go without us."

Don Farlow followed them down the long hallway towards the haunted room, glancing into each room they passed, stopping every now and then to check the view from the windows. In the room next to the haunted room the rug had been replaced over the hatch to the dungeon. They pulled it aside. A few minutes later the curate was in the cave, standing as close to the mouth as the reaching waters permitted, gazing out over the ocean. The sea had calmed considerably.

When he climbed back up, he was quite flushed with excitement. "Wow!" he said, as he turned. "What a find. This will put Panraven on the historic map when it all comes out in Mr. Peters' book. Thanks for your help, Susan and Glen. I can find my own way back. You'll want to get back to the piano. No doubt we'll meet again."

He watched them go until they were out of sight, then he ducked into one of the rooms. He was surprised to find the window already unlocked, and could easily be opened from outside. He frowned. Did someone else have the same idea?

It was a very thoughtful man who turned and headed for the outdoors. Nothing would happen in the daylight. He was sure of that.

Chapter Eleven

AFTER DINNER IN the great dining hall, Glen, Ding and Susan retired to the games room. Lucy was permitted to spend some time with them before having to leave to catch up on some of her work. It was approaching midnight when they decided to retire. Ding left to go to his room. Glen hesitated at the bottom of the stairs leading to the servants' bedrooms. A glance out the window had revealed a velvet sky, moonless but star-studded.

"It looks like a beautiful night, Susan. Would you like to go for a walk before we turn in?"

"Yes, let's. Just a minute while I fetch a cardigan."

Walking close together, they headed instinctively towards the clifftop. The wind that had buffeted them earlier had died to a whisper but they could still hear the waves rolling into the cave beneath them. They seemed to be abating reluctantly.

"I would take a boat out in *this* sea," said Glen, "if I had to. Earlier I wouldn't have considered it."

"We might be able to rent a boat with an outboard tomorrow if you would like," she suggested. "There's a man in Polgarth who rents them out occasionally. Would you like that?"

"Yes. That sounds like fun."

They had reached the clifftop and stood close together. The white-topped waves rolled in, a phosphorescent symphony of light and shadow as if reflecting the light of the stars.

"We're never far from the sea, anywhere in England. Not by *your* standards, anyway. We holidayed at Bognor Regis on the English Channel twice. But I never really *saw* the sea till I came here. It's beautiful. And somehow terrifying."

"You've got it! Beautiful and terrifying. Tonight it's a bit of both." He stopped short. He frowned.

"Did you see that?"

"What? Did I see what?"

"A light. Out there. Just for a moment. Just a flash."

"Are you sure? I didn't see anything. D'you suppose there's a boat out there?"

"There must be. There aren't any lighthouses. It looked like it's from a signal lamp. But what's he signalling? Must have been accidental."

"No! Look there!" Susan was pointing, down over the cliff edge. For just a moment he saw it, a light dancing across the wave tops before it was extinguished. Briefly the darkness seemed intensified in contrast, then the light appeared again, a soft glow reaching out tentatively from the mouth of the cave!

"Someone's in the cave! That's odd, to say the least. I wonder what's going on."

She looked at him. "Something *is* going on. D'you think we should investigate?"

He hesitated. "It could be none of our business. But darn it, it's mighty queer. Yes! Let's investigate."

"All right." They started walking back towards the house. "It doesn't make sense. There's just the four of us and Peters and Don Farlow who know about the cave — at least about the fake dungeon entrance to it. Maybe there's still some people using the cave for smuggling. They could come by boat tonight. The storm has let up."

"But there's no way to get smuggled goods up from the cave except by the dungeon. Of course they could just store it there until it can be picked up at a more convenient time by boat. Yes, smugglers could be out there now signalling they have some contraband. Well, I think we should find out. Sir Godfrey should know about it if that's what this is all about." He hesitated. "Unless he does know and is still involved in the trade himself."

"I don't think so." Susan shook her head. "No, I'm sure not. But we won't let on to anyone till we've taken a look.

They strode quickly down the slope to the hall. Everyone had gone to bed by now. Although Penraven was on a lonely spot far from anything likely to be a target of enemy bombers, the blackout regulations were strictly adhered to. They eased their way in through the folds of blackout curtains.

"Wait here a minute," whispered Glen. "I'll slip up and get my flashlight. We better not put any lights on."

He rejoined her a few minutes later, lighting their way through to the west wing. They paused at the beginning of the long hallway, light doused. There was nothing. No light, no sign of life.

"Come on." In darkness they walked quickly until they came to the room where they had found the entrance to the dungeon. Susan tried the door, tentatively. It eased open.

The hatch in the floor had been pulled back. There was a faint light showing from the open shaft.

They crept to it, looked down, but could see only the small patch of floor at the foot of the ladder. They crouched there, listening intently.

For a moment they could hear nothing. Then came a faint sound that might have been that of a boat easing in to the cave. Then they heard a voice.

"That's Mr. Peters," said Susan, relieved. "Something to do

with his book. Recreating the smuggling days, probably. Let's go and see,"

Glen hesitated, but she didn't. She lowered herself down the ladder. He followed.

A startling sight met his eyes. An inflatable dinghy had been drawn up into the cave. Four sailors stood, two on each side. Another man, obviously an officer, was talking to Mr. Peters. It was the uniforms that were startling.

The sailors wore the uniform of the German navy! The officer wore the white cap that identified him as the commanding officer of a U-boat!

Glen stared, unbelieving. "What the blazes! Susan, wait . . ."

But she hadn't noticed the uniforms. She was walking towards them, unfazed.

For a moment Glen was about to turn and run, and raise the alarm. But he couldn't leave Susan. He started after her, suddenly aware that Peters had turned to face them, surprise on his face. And a gun in his hand.

"What are you two doing here?" he demanded.

"We saw the light from up on the cliff," said Susan, still not catching on. "What is happening? Are you . . . ?" Then she saw the gun. She stopped short. Glen bumped into her.

"Glen," she whispered, shaken. "He has a gun! Who are those people?"

"They're from a German U-boat. Right, Mr. Peters?" He forced his voice to sound casual. "What *is* going on?"

For a moment Peters said nothing to the two of them. He

spoke briefly to the officer in a strange tongue that Glen took to be German, then he turned to them.

"You were a big help to me in finding the dungeon and a safer way into the cave," he said, conversationally. "Otherwise I would have had to get here by boat and I'm no sailor. As it is I was able to be here to meet my friends as scheduled."

"Your friends? They're Germans."

"Ah well, so am I, actually. My name is Stein when I'm at home. Where I haven't been for some time. But *that* is about to change. I'm happy to say." He held the gun casually, but he was ready to aim it at a moment's notice. "I wonder what I should do about you two. Are you alone?"

"No," lied Glen. "Everyone's awake and they're right behind us."

Peters frowned, then shook his head. "Good try, but I don't believe you. You are very privileged, you two. You are about to witness the unveiling of the ultimate weapon. The weapon that will win the war for us — for Germany, that is. In fact you may very well be its first victims, though that is questionable."

"What are you talking about?" Susan's voice trembled. She clutched Glen's arm. She took a deep breath. Suddenly there was anger in her voice, a challenge. "Where is this weapon you're talking about?"

"Right there." He pointed to a metal, lidded box on the floor of the cave. It was not very big. Perhaps a two-foot cube. "It looks harmless, doesn't it?" he said casually. "It's not, believe me." He hesitated as the U-boat officer spoke to him, urgently. But he shook his head in reply, then turned to Glen and Susan.

"Captain Schultz says I should shoot you two, but he doesn't understand. I'm not going to do that because there's nothing you can do about it anyway. Let me explain. Inside this box is a very small explosive which was set some minutes ago to go off in half an hour." He checked his watch. "Make that twenty-five minutes now. Or less. When it does, it will blow the lid off and a million tiny flying bugs will be released. Each one of those bugs thirsts for human blood and each one is infected with the bubonic plague."

They stared at him in horrified disbelief. This was what Sir Godfrey feared. And now it was a reality. The magnitude of the planned disaster was beyond comprehension.

"The plague!" said Glen, faintly. "You can't be serious."

"Oh yes, I am. The plague that killed millions in the Middle Ages and is just as deadly today."

"But I don't understand," said Susan bewildered. "Why? To win the war? But it will spread to Germany too."

"No," said Peters patiently, apparently enjoying himself. "They won't fly over any large body of water — such as the English Channel or the North Sea. You see what will happen. When they are released they will head in three directions towards fresh air. The cave mouth, of course. Out the mouth then into the air and spread inland. Some no doubt will find their way up through the dungeon. But there's an even better way. You may not know it but in the shadows behind you there are small fissures through which they will sense fresh air. Those openings lead into mine shafts from the old tin mining days, shafts that lead into other shafts and to the 'Cornish castles' you see dominating the skylines all over the place. Expressways to carry the plague far inland. In a few hours it will reach Plymouth. In a day or two, London. And they reproduce in flight! It is the ultimate weapon Hitler promised would win the war."

"I don't believe it," said Glen desperately. "No one would do such a thing." The trouble was that he *did* believe it. "If they won't fly over water they won't reach our troops on the continent, and we're winning."

"True," acknowledged Peters, "but your troops will never get any reinforcements and without them they'll eventually run out of men and supplies. Our troops can hold them until you have to give up."

"But it will leave Britain a wasteland. What good will that be to you? And it will spread worldwide. You won't be able to stop it. You can't start such a thing. It will never stop."

But Peters wasn't listening. He turned to the officer and spoke a few words, then turned back again. "The lid is going to blow off in — I'd say about twenty minutes. I don't know what you will do. Go up and try to waken the household? Throw it out the cave mouth into the sea?" He shook his head. "Believe it or not that box will float, thanks to a cork bottom. You will only have twenty minutes. Face it, you have no hope. Wherever you move it to, the bugs are still going to escape. I'm leaving you alive because I hope you live long enough — the plague doesn't kill instantly — to let everyone know where the little beauties came from. That Hitler has lived up to his promise of the ultimate weapon."

He turned to the sailors. "Let's go," he said. "*We* don't want to be the first victims of those bugs. Let's go home." They pushed the dinghy into the water. The officer climbed aboard, followed by Peters. As they pushed off into the darkness he waved. "Twenty minutes," he reminded them. "No, perhaps eighteen now. Eighteen minutes to contemplate disaster. And nothing you can do to prevent it."

Chapter Twelve

"EIGHTEEN MINUTES. Seventeen? We've got a problem." The voice came from *behind* them.

Glen and Susan spun around. Don Farlow was standing in the shadows at the foot of the dungeon ladder.

"Don!" gasped Susan. "You . . . you heard?"

"Everything," nodded Don grimly. "We've got to do something fast. You know that." They noticed him slip a gun into his pocket.

"You could have shot Peters," cried Susan. "Why didn't you?"

"Because you two would have been dead before he ever hit the floor. Every one of those men was armed. Never mind him. Leave him for God to deal with. Now, any ideas what we can do with this thing?" As he spoke he led them over to look down on the box touching it tentatively with his foot.

"You heard him," muttered Glen. "There's nothing we can do."

"If that's your attitude, you're quite right. I say there must be something we can do, or why are we here? I don't believe in chance. We've been given fifteen minutes. We have to use them."

"Oh!" Glen gulped. How could this man, whoever he really was, have any hope? He leaned down to touch the box hesitantly, pushing it, aware of the explosive inside. But it wasn't set to go off, not yet. He hefted it tentatively. It was not heavy. Of course not. A million tiny bugs don't weigh much. "We could get them upstairs, if that would do any good."

"Into the *house*?" Susan was incredulous.

"Into the cupboard," said Glen. "And seal the doors." But he knew, even as he said it, that it was a hopeless suggestion.

But Don was encouraging. "That would delay things," he said. "But that's all. We must do more."

"Smoke," suggested Susan, tightly. "If we could fill the cupboard somehow with smoke it might smother the bugs."

"Now you're talking," Don said. "That's the first thing. Let's get them up the ladder. Smoke alone wouldn't be the whole answer of course. Lots of them would get away. There

has to be something else. Get up top, Glen, and I'll hand the
box up to you."

A thought occurred to Glen. "Susan," he said suddenly,
"have you any petrol?" He felt sure the answer was no, since
he had heard they always used the horse and cart, not the
car.

But she surprised him. "Yes. There's always some in case
of emergency. In the garage."

"Then get it," urged Don, understanding immediately.
"We've got ten minutes. Get it back here. If you should see a
rope, bring that too but don't waste time looking for one.
Go."

Susan hesitated, bewildered. Then she fled.

Did they really think they could prevent this tragedy from
happening? Petrol? That suggested fire. How do you set a
metal box on fire? Hope and doubt fought each other, but
they had to do something . . .

Susan ran down the darkened hallway, though the doorway
into the central wing, across the wide reception room, into
the servants' quarters, her mind a turmoil. A rope? What on
earth could he do with a rope? She had no idea where she
would find one without going into the barn, and there was
no time for that. Forget the rope. He wanted petrol. She
wasn't sure why. Surely a metal box was fireproof. But he
must have *some* scheme in mind. Hers not to ask why.

She pushed impatiently through the blackout curtains.

There was a faint light from the sky outside. She dashed across the yard towards the black shape of the garage. There was petrol in there. How come the yard was suddenly so wide? It seemed to take forever just to reach the garage door. Precious seconds were slipping away. She grasped the door handle. It was locked!

Locked, from the inside. Just a bolt, she thought, that would have to be slipped back. There was a door in the back of the garage leading to Jake's upstairs quarters. But there was no time to rouse Jake and try to explain what was going on. She had to get in there. There was a window. Low enough to climb through. And there was a spade, leaning against the wall. She had never seen one there before. Somehow its presence raised her hopes. She lifted it up and brought it down and smashed through the glass with a terrific noise.

Jake must hear that. But there was no time to worry. In the pale light she noticed shards of glass still clinging to the window frame. She swept the spade around the circumference, hoping that would get rid of the glass. She hoisted herself up, pushing her torso through the opening, barely aware that she had *not* gotten rid of all the glass. Something bit into her hands, ripped her clothing. Ignoring it, kicking her legs, pushing with her bleeding hands, she finally fell though, landing on her shoulder, rolling.

It was dark, of course, the two autos merely darker shapes in the blackness. But she knew where the petrol can was kept. Pray God it would still be there. She groped her way to the corner. Yes. There it was, a gallon can. Not full. Maybe half. That would have to do, and it would be easier to carry than a full can.

She reached the door, groped for the bolt, aware of shouting from overhead, the sound of footsteps on the stair behind. For a moment the bolt stuck. Blood-soaked hands slipped on it. Gritting her teeth she wiped her hands on her cardigan, tried again. The bolt slid back. She pushed the door open, ran towards the house.

Lights were on upstairs. As she pushed through the blackout curtains she heard someone pounding down the stairs. Through the curtains, across the kitchen heading for the door into the central wing . . .

"Susan. What the hell . . . " It was Ding, staring at her, at the petrol can in her hands.

She just shook her head and ran on, across the foyer again, now with Ding coming after her, calling out. Into the west wing, the long corridor stretching before her. She could see a light at the end, a light in the room next to the haunted room. Glen and Don must be in there. Was she in time? And if she was, what could they do . . . ?

Once Susan had left, Glen and Don had sprung into action, manhandling the box up the ladder. Don took the lead now. "Into the cupboard with it. Is there carpet on the floor in there? No? All right, we'll do it out here. Rip up the carpet and wrap it around the box."

Glen grabbed a corner of the carpet, pulling against the glue that held it down. Don had a knife. He was ripping it apart as Glen loosened it, wrapping it around the box. Time was running out. At any moment now the explosive would release the bugs.

"Peters said it's just a minor explosive, didn't he?" Don gasped out. "If we can keep the lid on, we'll cook 'em and kill the virus or whatever it is. We're going to set the whole room on fire so if any do escape they'll burn. That is, if Susan can find some petrol. Which probably means setting the whole house ablaze." He grimaced. "It's called 'overkill.' Anyway, it's our only hope. Otherwise we've failed. We need something to put on top to hold it. If we had a rope . . . but we haven't." He looked around. "That chair," he said. "That will have to do. I wonder how accurate those twenty minutes are that our friend Peters mentioned. We've just about run out of time. Where's Susan . . . ?"

"I'm here!" She was there, gasping, bloody, holding out the petrol can.

"Good girl!" He saw the blood on her hands and torn clothing. His eyes widened but there was no time.

"Right. Stand back. We're going to set this whole room ablaze." Don splashed gasoline over the piled carpet, then over the floor, even the walls.

"Now." He laid a trail of petrol out the door, shut it, then continued the trail for a few more feet. He ran out of petrol. He took a match from his pocket.

"All right. Get out of here. Waken everyone. Make sure everyone's out. And call the fire brigade. By the time they get here those little beauties will either be burned up or we'll have the worst plague on record about to wipe out half the population of Britain."

He struck the match, held it to the trail of petrol, watched it for a moment as it licked its way rapidly towards the closed door. Then he too turned and ran.

They were at the door to the central wing when there was a gigantic *whoosh*, the door to the room burst open and a wall of flame erupted, lurid, fierce, angry.

"I guess," said Glen, as they ran, "we've solved Sir Godfrey's problem for him — what to do with the west wing."

Chapter Thirteen

THE DINGHY, LIGHT doused, had crawled like a black spider towards the waiting submarine. Jim Peters had a brief glimpse of Glen's flashlight in the cave, then it was gone and he could see only the cliff, a darker mass outlined by the star-lit sky. Penraven House was lost in the void behind it.

What was going on there? The boy and girl must be frantic, he thought. What would they do? Probably try to waken everyone and hope someone had some idea what to do, but there would be no time. He glanced at his watch. Three minutes to go. Although their appearance in the cave had startled him, he was glad now that the sailor and the girl had been there. They were witnesses to the fact that the plague was indeed the work of the Nazis, that their *Führer* had come through as promised . . .

Sooner than he expected, the conning tower of the submarine was looming above him. At the captain's urging he climbed the ladder to the bridge, followed by the skipper while the men deflated and stowed the dinghy. Up here the black bulk of Penraven House was visible. The captain handed him a pair of binoculars.

"I tell you, Herr Peters or Stein or whatever your name is, I am glad to be rid of that cargo. I had no idea what it was. Frankly, I don't like it. Germ warfare? That's not war, it's murder."

Jim Peters laughed. He was feeling elated at his victory. "Too dishonourable for you? Too underhanded? That's what they used to say about submarines, remember?"

The captain grunted. "We fight against men and ships and nations, not against women and children."

"Where have you been hiding, Captain? Civilians of all ages and genders are fair game in this war. How would you prefer to die? In bed from the plague or burned to death in a firestorm from the sky? That's what's happening in Hamburg where your boat came from. Anyway, it's all academic now. Those bugs were freed five minutes ago. The plague is about to begin. You know the old saying. 'The end justifies the means.'"

"I don't . . ." The captain broke off. He was staring at the house. "There! Did you see that? A light at one of the windows. A flame . . ."

"A flame? No. Impossible. The house is blacked out." But he sounded uneasy. Then — "*Oh mein Gott!*"

Fire. There was no doubt about it. "They've set the whole house on fire. But they're too late. They must be. The bugs were down in the cave. Fire won't reach them there."

"They could take them up, couldn't they? The kids were too smart for you. Somehow they've set fire to the whole house to make sure! I told you to shoot them while you had the chance! *Mein Gott*, Stein. I would hate to be in your shoes when the High Command hears you've failed."

"I haven't failed!" Peters sounded desperate. "We don't know for sure. They may be too late . . ."

"You hope." The captain sounded almost amused. "Well there's nothing else you can do now *but* hope . . ."

He was interrupted. A voice called out from below.

"Hydrophones have picked up an echo, sir. Sounds like a destroyer. Moving fast. This way."

"Very well. Prepare to dive."

The captain touched Jim Peters on the shoulder. "Let's go. This is my war now. Either I avoid this destroyer or neither of us will have to worry about facing the High Command or any one else."

Chapter Fourteen

"YOU'RE NOT REALLY a curate, are you?"

Susan, Glen and Ding had taken refuge in St. Mark's Parish hall while the fire department fought to save what they could of Penraven, and Don Farlow faced difficult questions from the police, the firemen and a bewildered Sir Godfrey Trevour.

The supposed curate had arrived at last, to tell the three that a long telephone conversation with officials from the Defence Department and Army Intelligence had persuaded everyone concerned, without details, that the west wing, at least, had been sacrificed in an effort to avoid a terrible tragedy.

"I don't know how much of what went on will be made public," said a tired looking Don Farlow. "Or if your part in it will ever be known. That's up to someone else, thank God. The censors will have a field day trying to decide if the public should be notified now or later, or if ever. If everyone knew to what length the Nazis are willing to go to avoid defeat it might cause panic. However — " He dismissed the problem with a wave of his hand.

"To get to your question, Susan, no, I'm not a curate. That was a disguise to manufacture a reason to explore Penraven House. You see, we had an agent working undercover in the Nazis' laboratories working on germ warfare. He knew that something desperate was being planned and tried to get in touch with one of our men, but apparently he was unmasked and killed, but not before he got a garbled message through. The only word that was clear was "Penraven.""

"I was sent down here to find out what I could about Penraven. The most obvious thing was the cave that had once been used in smuggling, and was open to the ocean. That suggested several things. I was wondering how to get in to the cave, preferably in secret, when you, along with our friend who calls himself Peters, discovered the bottle dungeon and its access to the cave. I guess you know the rest."

"And you think the fire destroyed the . . . the bugs, or whatever they were?"

"Oh yes. The firemen discovered the remains of the containers. As Peters said, they were fireproof, but they were open, and *anything* that was inside them was obliterated."

"That's a relief. Do you suppose they will try again? Somewhere else?"

"I doubt it. This was a one-time effort. No one wants to play around with the bubonic plague. It's pretty certain that they destroyed their remaining stock in case it got loose among their own people. This was it. And thanks to you, it failed."

"And you. We would have been helpless if you hadn't been there," said Glen.

"That's true," nodded Don. "It took the three of us. As I think I said at the time, I don't believe in chance. We were put there for a reason."

"I've wondered about Peters," said Susan. "It's a shame he got away, even though his plan failed."

Don grinned. "You know what I like to think? That the U-boat was still on the surface when the fire took hold, that Peters saw it, and realized that his plan failed. *That* would be vengeance enough for me. Now, what about you two sailors. I think you deserve another Survivor's Leave. Don't you?"

"Oh no!" said Ding with feeling. "I'm looking forward to a nice long sea voyage with nothing to fear but U-boats and Japanese kamikazes at the end of it. Don't you agree, Glen?"

"Well, I don't know. Actually, all things considered, this was a pretty darn good leave." He was thinking of two blue eyes and dark midnight brown hair with auburn highlights.

A few days later they were standing on the platform waiting for the tank engine with its ancient coaches to arrive. "I'm sorry you aren't going to meet Jack and Heather," said Susan. "You have to get back to base, do you?"

"I have two days left of leave but I promised my dad I would get up to Scotland to visit his birthplace so, yes, I have to go. After that, I don't know. That's up to the navy. Maybe I'll have a chance later, but not likely. I expect to be heading for the Pacific on our new aircraft carrier before long." He hesitated, looking at her. "You know what Don Farlow said. He doesn't believe in chance. Well, neither do I. Meeting you was more than mere chance."

The shrill cry of the approaching train rent the air. He looked around. "Where's Ding."

"Over there," she said. "Kissing Lucy goodbye."

"Good for him. He has the right idea." He held out his arms. She came to him. "But it's not goodbye, is it? We'll meet again?"

"Oh yes."

ABOUT THE AUTHOR

Born in Priceville, Ontario, in 1925, Robert Sutherland lived briefly in Cape Breton and then Scotland before returning to Canada where he attended Flesherton High School in Ontario. During World War II, he joined the Royal Canadian Navy and served from 1943 to 1946 as an anti-aircraft gunner on a Loch Class frigate (HMCS *Loch Morlich*). When his ship was in dry dock in London for repairs, he experienced Doodlebug bombing. While in the navy he met Charlotte Cameron of Glasgow, and they married in Toronto in 1948. They have three children, seven grandchildren and one great-grandson. Robert's first success with fiction was a full length novel in the *Toronto Star Weekly* in 1960. He used the proceeds to set up a hobby of selling Scottish regalia and gifts from his home, a hobby he still pursues. On two of his many rejection slips for other novels, the editor had written "Suggest you try writing for teens." When he returned to writing in the1980s he decided to follow this advice. He rewrote the story that had been published in the *Star*, cutting down on the descriptions and making his protagonist a teen who accidentally stumbled into espionage. *Mystery at Black Rock Island*, published by Scholastic, was an immediate success, and the first of five successful books about teenagers David and Sandy. He has now had fourteen novels published, which have received numerous nominations and prizes. His novels have been translated into French, Norwegian, Swedish, German and Korean. Robert now lives in Westport, Ontario.

Recycled
Supporting responsible use
of forest resources
www.fsc.org Cert no. SGS-COC-003153
© 1996 Forest Stewardship Council

Marquis Book Printing Inc.

Québec, Canada
2009

This book has been printed on 100% post consumer
waste paper, certified Eco-logo and processed chlorine free.